Revenge

King Crawley had a taste of it—but it wasn't enough to slake his thirst for vengeance. As it had once before, the Seattle racketeer's evil snaked out like tentacles, to wrap around an unsuspecting victim....

This time the sins of the father would be visited on the son. This time there could be no escape for Dakota Raferty— or for the father he idolized.

King Crawley's weapon was the most powerful force on earth....

A mother's love for her child.

There is one more victim on King Crawley's list— Asia Raferty. Her story is next in Intrigue #165 NO HOLDS BARRED.

For Crawley, revenge is sweet....

Dear Reader:

The idea of writing a series of connected mysteries has intrigued me for years. My opportunity and greatest challenge came with the idea for QUID PRO QUO. While the books are interconnected, each story not only stands on its own, but is different from the others in setting and style. You'll go from the Oregon coast to the Olympic peninsula, from psychological suspense to action adventure. During your travels, I hope you'll enjoy sharing danger and romance with Benno and Sydney, Dakota and Honor, and Dominic and Asia as much as I did while creating their stories.

Follow King Crawley's final quest for revenge next month in Intrigue #165 *No Holds Barred*.

—Patricia Rosemoor

Squaring Accounts

Patricia Rosemoor

Harlequin Books

TORONTO • NEW YORK • LONDON
AMSTERDAM • PARIS • SYDNEY • HAMBURG
STOCKHOLM • ATHENS • TOKYO • MILAN

To Wal—hope this keeps you up all night

Harlequin Intrigue edition published June 1991

ISBN 0-373-22163-0

SQUARING ACCOUNTS

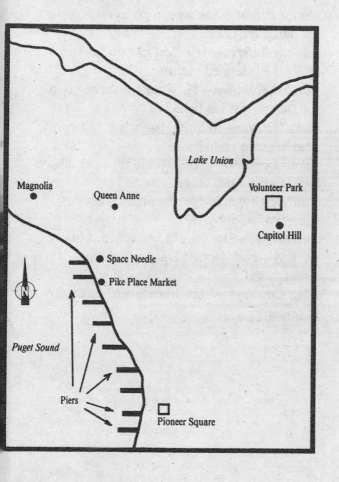

Magnolia

Queen Anne

Lake Union

Volunteer Park

Capitol Hill

Space Needle

Pike Place Market

N

Puget Sound

Piers

Pioneer Square

CAST OF CHARACTERS

Honor Bright—She would do *anything* to get her daughter back.

Dakota Raferty—He didn't know he was really the intended victim.

Willard Zahniser—How far would he go to get Dakota off his back?

Gary Webster—Would Honor's ex-husband steal his own child?

Karen Lopinski—The tabloid reporter always looking for a hot story.

Andrew Vaughn—He resented Dakota's success as a lobbyist.

Janet Ingel—She fought her way out of poverty—and wanted Dakota's privileged background.

King Crawley—What harm could he do in prison?

Prologue

"Mommy, can we see the mountains with the telescope?" Nora Bright Webster asked as she peered out at them from the Space Needle observation deck.

Glancing at snow-capped Mount Rainier in the southeast, Honor tugged one of her four-year-old's copper braids. "Sure we can, peaches."

The brilliance of Nora's smile was contagious. "Yea! I like the mountains." Green eyes too large for her small face sparkled; peaches-and-cream cheeks lightly sprinkled with freckles glowed. "We don't never have to go back to California or those other places, do we?"

Taking her gaze away from the tiny miniature of herself, Honor opened her purple leather clutch to get coins for the pay telescope. "Not for a long time, anyway."

A small child needed stability, and another year or two would probably seem like forever to her. Though they'd been in Seattle for eleven months, Nora still had to be reassured that her latest home and her newest friends wouldn't be snatched away from her as they had been so frequently in the past.

Honor was digging for her coin purse when she was jostled from behind. The clutch tumbled from her hands, spilling its contents over the floor. With a sound of exasperation, she slid her slim lilac skirt high enough to allow her to stoop. Gathering the dozen or so loose items, she scooped them back into her purse. She only had her back to her daughter for a few seconds, but when she rose and turned, Nora was gone, no doubt having wandered off into the crowd.

"Nora, honey, where are you?"

Frowning, Honor stepped toward the core of the observation tower and searched the throng of tourists— some waiting to leave, others milling about. Then the doors of the elevator slid open. Even more people surged out of the car, driving her back.

"Nora!" she called again.

As she looked around in vain, her concern quickly grew.

Telling herself to stay calm, Honor began circling the tower. She assured herself that Nora was fine, that her daughter must have gotten swept up by the crowd, that she would spot her at any second. But halfway around the observation deck, she realized she should have caught up to her daughter by now. Her pulse threaded unevenly. A large knot of tourists loomed before her, threatening to slow her down. She shoved through them, mumbling her apologies.

But no matter how fast she went, she couldn't catch sight of Nora.

Heart thundering in fear, Honor stopped near the elevator boarding area. She'd come full circle for nothing. What now? she wondered, fighting to think clearly.

She had to get help.

But before she could place one purple pump in front of the other, a hard body pressed full length against her back and a large hand gripped her elbow.

"Don't turn around, Ms. Bright."

The low, hoarse words whispered at her ear were menacing. The breath caught in her throat, and Honor did as she was told. He knew who she was—and she wasn't stupid.

"Nora . . . where is she?" Honor swallowed hard and choked out, "And what is it you want?"

"I want you to read this."

A folded piece of white paper flew past her. Before she could grab the note, the elevator doors opened and a new set of tourists poured out, one stepping on the missive and kicking it back, farther out of Honor's reach. More people got between her and the note. Nearly in a frenzy, she pushed into their midst.

"Get out of my way!" she yelled, desperate to get her hands on the lifeline to her daughter.

"Geez, lady!" a teenager complained.

"How rude!" an elderly woman added.

Their words barely registering, Honor lunged for the note, scraping her shins and tearing a stocking as she hit the deck. Her trembling fingers snatched the folded paper from the threat of an oncoming foot. Still on her knees, she pressed the paper to her chest for a second. She was trembling all over and couldn't stop.

Finally, she unfolded the note and read it.

Tell no one if you want to see your daughter again.
Go home and wait for instructions.

Her pulse came in quick little spurts and her head

grew light as she looked around for the man who'd left the message. Not that she could recognize him. Dazed, she let her eyes slide over a half dozen men before returning to the words already emblazoned on her mind.

A uniformed security guard approached. "You okay, ma'am?"

She blinked stupidly. "Yes, I . . ."

His hand tucked under her arm and he lifted her to her feet. "Come on, we'll find you a place to sit."

"No. No! I have to go home."

"Rest for a minute, first," he said kindly.

"No! Right now!"

"Okay, okay." He let go of her and backed off. "Whatever you say, ma'am."

Whatever you say.

Honor wanted to say her daughter had been kidnapped and beg the security guard to help her. He'd probably think she was crazy like the rest of the people who'd stopped to watch.

And if *they* found out she'd told. . . .

Her stomach clutched and threatened to empty. Honor clasped her hand over her mouth and took a shaky breath. She willed herself to breathe normally. To smile. It was the greatest job of acting she'd ever done.

For Nora was her heart. Her life. Without her daughter, Honor had nothing.

"I'm all right. Really," she assured the security guard, who stood staring, his expression concerned as she edged toward the elevator. "I just have to go home now. I'm all right."

A lie. If anything happened to Nora . . .

As she slipped the note into her clutch and pulled out her key ring, Honor feared that she might never be all right again.

Chapter One

Eight o'clock and all would be well if only the Public Interest Lobbying Cooperative offices would empty of the extra people that weren't supposed to be there!

While peering down the hall from the doorway of the ladies lounge for the hundredth time in the past hour, Honor heard raised voices. She drew back and watched the glass reflection via the darkened office across the way.

A man and a woman exited PILC without locking the door behind them. Someone else was still inside, then. She had to work fast or she'd be out of luck—when the last person left, she'd be locked out with no way to get what she needed.

Honor's knees grew weak at the thought of her next bold move.

The couple rounded the corner and a second later, Honor heard the grinding whir of old machinery as the elevator ascended to the fifth floor. A loud clunk and a ding signaled the car's arrival.

She drew back into the lounge that spanned the center hub. Another door on the opposite side of the room lead to a second corridor. The old building was a complex maze, but as far as she'd been able to tell, the security system was simple, and a single guard was stationed at street level with a sign-out book. Unwilling to chance the guard recognizing her when she left later, Honor had brought a few items to change her appearance. Her disguise was packed in a tote bag that she now hid behind one of several padded chairs.

Then she made her move.

Pulse racheting through her, Honor slipped down the hall and approached the lobbyists' offices. Her plan *had* to work. She was no burglar. She didn't know how to jimmy locks and bypass alarms. She'd told *them* that—for all the good it had done her. She'd lain awake the night before and had frazzled her brain coming up with a plan.

Pretending she was part of a messenger service, she'd called PILC earlier that afternoon to find out if someone would be working late. Supposedly, she needed to drop off a packet of materials for one of the lobbyists. She'd been told someone would be around until eight or so. She hadn't expected *several* someones.

Please let it be only one person left, Honor prayed as she stepped near the door. One busy, overworked person who wouldn't catch her coming in.

She took a good look through the window in the door. No one was in the spacious outer work area with its half dozen desks. So far, so good. A light in one of the inner offices caught her eye. A dark-haired woman was pulling a book from a shelf and seemed to be totally absorbed.

Grateful the outer door opened silently, Honor slipped inside the main room while quickly searching for a place to hide. She had a choice. She could either fold herself into a pretzel and wait under a desk, or she could try the nearest door and hope it was unlocked.

Hearing the woman moving about again, Honor chose the door and found herself in a supply closet. Like a contortionist, she squeezed inside and managed to prop herself awkwardly against a stack of boxes. Sequestered in the dark with only a blur of light at floor level to keep her company, she strained to listen through the solid walnut door as the woman's heels clacked closer.

Honor's skin went clammy and she thought she would be sick. What if the woman needed something from the supply closet and found her? Even if she got away, she might be recognized! The heels stopped and a chair creaked, the screech competing with the pounding of her heart. A few seconds later, the woman's voice drifted into Honor's hiding place.

"Steffie, how are things going at your end?"

Honor drew in some fetid air—a short, sharp breath that rocked her stomach. The other woman was on the telephone. For how long? she wondered. She could hardly wait for this to be over. She'd never done anything illegal before.

"I'm going to talk to the other lobbyists about it tomorrow," the woman assured Steffie.

She was doing this for Nora, Honor reminded herself. Whoever *they* were hadn't wanted money as ransom, and she would do anything to get her daughter back safe and sound. Nothing else mattered. Not even the identities of the people who held Nora captive. Honor didn't want to know who they were. All she wanted was Nora.

"Helping women and their kids is going to be my top personal priority," the lobbyist was saying.

Women and their kids.

Her and Nora.

She clenched her jaw and made fists, digging her nails into her palms. She had to stop this, had to stop thinking about Nora or she would be a basket case, unable to carry through with her mission. Then how would she be able to free her daughter? She had to keep her mind on her plan.

By the time the dark-haired woman finished her conversation with Steffie, Honor was sweating.

By the time the woman packed up her things and left—the light illuminating the crack at the floor went black—Honor was shaking.

Yet Honor waited. Counted to one hundred. Then she eased the door open, and once assured she was alone, burst through into the dark office with a sob of relief.

She needed the little fresh air the open room provided, sucked it in greedily for all the good it did her. Never before so nervous and sick to her stomach, she didn't have time to coddle herself, not with the stakes so high. She forced herself to move, to do exactly as the kidnappers had instructed.

Her hand shook as she unzipped the belt pack at her waist and found the mini mag light she'd stored inside. She moved to the nearest office and flashed the beam over the nameplate on the door that was cracked open. Too bad it was the wrong office. She repeated the process, only finding the right name on the third try.

Dakota Raferty.

How she hated to do this, especially to him. But it wasn't a question of fairness. She had no choice. She jiggled the handle, but his door, of course, was locked.

"Damn!" she whispered in frustration. "I knew this would happen. I just knew it!"

She'd come prepared with her little kit—the best she could do considering she was a rank amateur. In addition to the light, she'd stored various other objects that she'd thought might be of use in the belt pack. The screwdriver did her no good in trying to jimmy the lock. She'd brought a tool that would etch glass and make it easier to break, but this door had no window except for the one in the transom.

She stared up at the rectangular piece of glass approximately one and a half by three feet. Big enough to slide through.

Knowing there was no helping it, she flashed her small light around. The desks and filing cabinets were all old, solid wood and very heavy. Thank goodness she'd never been a woman who relied on a man to do everything for her—and that she lifted weights as part of her exercise program. She stepped to the nearest desk and found that she could cajole it forth a few inches at a time without making too much noise in case anyone was around to hear, which was unlikely.

She hoped.

Five minutes later, the desk barricaded the office door. She climbed to the raised surface quickly, thankful she'd dressed sensibly in spandex tights, a thigh-length, loose top and flat shoes. She could easily get at the transom now, but pulling herself up and through without cutting herself on broken glass could be another problem altogether.

Luckily, she might not have to break the glass at all, Honor realized.

The transom was open a crack!

Placing the flashlight in her teeth and aiming it so she could see what she was doing, Honor used the screwdriver to get at the catch on the other side of the door. No leverage. Climbing down, she found a sturdy four-legged chair and placed it in the middle of the desk. That gave her too much height, so she worked hunched over until she was able to open the transom several inches and reveal the hinges.

The screws didn't want to budge, but Honor was determined. Finally, they worked free and, sticking the flashlight in the open belt pack, she dismantled the window. She was trying to balance the heavy wood and glass when she heard the elevator clunk to a stop.

Her head whipped around to look at the front door and she froze, window suspended in midair. A moment later, the guard peered in—he was obviously making his rounds. Honor's heart leapt to her throat as he gave the room a cursory pass with his flashlight. Either the man was near blind or he wasn't looking, because the beam illuminated her legs as it swept past.

Her burden was getting heavier by the second and the guard couldn't go on too soon for her peace of mind or muscle. Her arms were shaking, her wrists were ready to give way and her fingers were burning. When she thought she couldn't hold the weight any longer, he moved away. Hesitating only a second, she pulled the window toward her.

Wood clunked against wood as frame met door jamb. Honor felt instant relief as the stress left her arms. She readjusted the weight but paused a moment to make sure the guard hadn't heard. He was probably deaf as well as blind, she thought wryly, because he didn't come back. She guessed he was circling the entire floor and, if she were lucky, he would approach the elevators from the other direction.

Please let me be lucky, for Nora's sake, if not my own!

Carefully pulling the frame through the opening, Honor set the window on the desk so it was leaning against the wall. She poked her head through to the inner office and used the flashlight to make sure her descent would be clear. Nothing in the way.

With an adrenaline rush, she slipped through the opening and sat long enough to get her balance. Then she turned over so she was waist to the jamb, got a good grip with both hands and let herself down easily, front sliding against the door. She dropped the final couple of feet to the floor with ease, then sagged with relief, forehead pressed into the wood.

She'd done it. Thank God. Everything would be okay now.

Nora would be all right. If she found the correct information, Honor reminded herself, wondering why the kidnappers had chosen *her* for such a task. *They* were the professionals.

Thinking she could use more than the flashlight and still be safe, she turned on a desk lamp and aimed it at the file cabinets. She opened the drawer marked R-V and was somewhat amazed when the correct hanging file seemed to jump out at her: Salmon Fishing Industry.

After all she'd been through to get this far, finding the file in its proper place seemed laughingly easy. Not about to question her luck, however, Honor grabbed the documents and slid the drawer closed. A responding sound seemed to come from the next room. Honor quickly switched off the light and listened intently in case the guard had returned.

Silence.

Her imagination? Or an echo of her own activity bouncing through acoustically poor rooms?

Neither option threatening, she moved to the door, her mind on escape. First return things the way she found them. Replacing the window would be a piece of cake, and hopefully, the door would automatically lock behind her. Then all she had to do was move the desk back into place to be practically home free. Rather Nora would be, Honor thought, visualizing her reunion with her daughter.

One step closer to that goal, she opened the door only to freeze yet again.

There, on the other side of the desk, illuminated by the beam of her flashlight, stood a tall, broad-shouldered blond-haired man wearing a pin-striped suit . . . and a very dangerous expression.

"WHO THE HELL ARE YOU, and what do you want?" Dakota Raferty demanded as he was nearly blinded by the light shining in his face.

Giving no answer, the person clicked off the flashlight and made a furtive dart forward to shove at something. Dakota put out his hands in self-defense as a window came flying at him. He caught it by the frame and shoved it back against the wall as the dark-clad figure zigzagged in the other direction and scrambled over the edge of the desk.

"Oh, no, you don't!" he growled.

Knowing his size and strength to be superior, Dakota tackled the would-be thief, determined that he would teach the fellow that crime didn't pay!

But, as they went down to the tile floor together, Dakota felt full flesh under his hands that could only belong to a woman. A not-so-small-or-weak one at that! She was tall and strong and determined. She fought him with everything she had even while trying to hold on to whatever she'd broken into his office to get.

Even so, Dakota took the advantage of his greater size, swinging a leg over her body to pin her. He grasped her wrists and jerked. Her prize slipped away with the woosh of papers being strewn across the floor.

"Who are you and what were you trying to steal?" he demanded, dragging her hands up over her head and pinning them to the floor.

He was straddling his captive, holding her hips firmly in place with his knees. Her flesh was luxurious but tightly muscled—the proof of which he felt as she heaved and tried to buck him off—and he figured she was into fitness training.

"You can answer me . . . or the police," he threatened when her furious silence continued.

Abruptly, she stopped struggling. "All right," she finally said, her voice low and husky and filled with emotion he recognized as panic. "Let me up and I'll tell you."

"How about if you tell me and then maybe I'll think about letting you up."

He had the upper hand and might have kept to the threat if a sob hadn't caught in her throat. And she was trembling under him. She couldn't hide her fear.

Served her right, he thought, telling himself not to soften just because she was a woman.

Despite the self-admonishment, Dakota rose. He was careful to keep his right hand firmly wrapped around her wrist, however. He tugged none too gently—she was a thief, after all, afraid or not—and dragged her to the wall where he threw on a light switch.

What greeted his gaze took him aback.

"I know you," he said, inspecting familiar green eyes, porcelain complexion and flawless features revealed by copper hair drawn back into a French braid. "Don't I?"

She blinked and he could see the truth of his words in her eyes. Then her expression changed subtly.

"Sure you do. I'm a friend of Marc Lucas," she explained, naming one of Dakota's fellow lobbyists. "We met briefly at a party several months ago."

Dakota knew that to be a lie. Marc had only been with PILC for six weeks, and they'd never met before that.

"A party," he echoed, playing along, wondering how far she'd try to take him. She was a striking woman with a body to match, and he suspected she wouldn't hesitate to use whatever she thought would work to con him. His guard doubled. "I'm sure I would remember you."

"You said you knew me."

"But I forgot your name."

He could tell she was thinking quickly before she answered, "Sandy Mitchell. Marc wanted to play a practical joke on you and I was helping him out."

"Try again."

"What do you mean?"

She was good. Her expression was somewhere between innocent and indignant. A great actress.

Actress.

That was it!

He visualized her with masses of rich copper-red curls brushing her high cheekbones as well as shoulders and perfect back, both bared by a scanty copper-colored evening gown or an even scantier bathing suit. He'd seen those commercials and magazine ads for Flawless products dozens of times—he'd had a personal interest in them because the cosmetic company was his sister's account.

"Honor Bright." He let go of her wrist. Now that he had her identity, he didn't need to hold her by force. The knowledge was enough to keep her in line until he got some answers. "We've never met before, but I recognize the face. Plus, I know my sister Syd set you up with work here in Seattle."

The situation was becoming even more puzzling. Could his younger sister have something to do with this fiasco? Dakota wondered, though he couldn't think of Sydney being involved in anything even slightly illegal after what she'd just been through.

Before he could probe, Honor said, "That's why I didn't want to do this. Because of Sydney, I mean."

She winced as she rubbed her wrist gingerly, making Dakota wonder if he'd really hurt her, though why he would care, he didn't know. Considering she had broken into his office—making him the victim of a crime in this situation—he was behaving quite reasonably.

"We're friends," Honor went on, "and I owe Sydney a lot. Not that I wanted to steal anything at all. You have to believe I was forced into this." Her forehead furled into a frown. "But why from you? It's so weird. I've been asking myself that all day."

She truly sounded as if she didn't know.

Dakota leaned back against a desk and crossed his arms over his pin-striped shirt. "Why me? Good question. Maybe if you tell me the truth about what's going on here, we can figure it out."

"What's going on is . . ."

Her voice faded indicating the intensity of her distress. He thought she was about to cry, but she pulled herself together and faced him with a neutral expression.

"Promise me no police," she said.

"Hey, I'm not promising anything. I don't have to. I can call the police anytime I want. Like now." He reached for the telephone.

"No, don't!" She caught his hand and her pleading gaze met his. "You win—all right? They said if I told anyone, she would die. You must remember that." She took a deep breath. "My daughter, Nora, has been kidnapped, so you can't call the police."

Her eyes filled with tears. Dakota couldn't tell whether the emotion was real or manufactured. Acting was Honor Bright's profession.

"How do I know you're not lying?"

She blinked and a single tear rolled down her cheek. She let go of his hand to brush the moisture away. "I guess trusting me is out of the question, right?"

Despite himself, Dakota was moved. He wanted to believe her. Only he couldn't quite manage such trust without more information.

"Who kidnapped your daughter?"

"I don't know. Yesterday we went to the Space Needle for a Sunday afternoon outing. We were having such a good time." She swallowed hard. "Then someone bumped into me and the contents of my purse scattered all over. I only turned my back to pick things up for a few seconds...but that was long enough. They got Nora out in that crowd right under my nose."

The tears were falling freely now and, studying her intently, Dakota could tell they weren't the first she'd shed. The skin around her eyes was puffy, and the whites were threaded with red. She'd been doing a lot of crying about something recently.

"What do they want?" he asked gruffly. She was touching his emotions whether he would allow her to or not.

"Not money. They wouldn't take my money. One of them called last night. The voice was synthesized—you know, electronically processed so I couldn't even tell if it was a man's or woman's. Whoever it was said I had to get my hands on classified information about your lobbying efforts concerning the salmon industry." She choked out a laugh. "My daughter for some information on fish. I don't understand."

But Dakota did. "That explains why they chose you, I guess, since you're the spokesperson for the Northwest Coast Salmon Council—the competition, such as it is."

For whatever reasons, Honor had left the fast lane of Hollywood. Sydney, who'd worked with Honor on the highly successful Flawless ad campaign, had suggested the NCSC job.

"What's so important about these files?"

"You don't need to know that."

The documents dealt with highly sensitive issues involving NCSC. Individuals' testimony and photos, evidence the council was whitewashing illegal salmon-fishing activities. Dakota would use the information in his lobbying effort to have stricter controls enacted. He hadn't figured the opposition had even known what he had.

"I never guessed someone would be willing to put a little girl in jeopardy and make her mother a criminal for these," he said, indicating the documents. And then, more firmly, "Finding the kidnappers is a job for the police."

"You can't call the police!" Honor cried, sounding as if she were fighting hysteria. "Nora's only a baby. Only four years old. I can't lose her."

"Professionals know how to handle—"

"No!" She grabbed on to his arm, her long nails pressing into his flesh through the fabric of his suit jacket. "Please, I'm begging you. Please!"

Honor was weeping openly now, and her sobs tore at Dakota's heart. And still he suspected she could be acting to get what she wanted. For God's sake, he didn't even know for certain if she had a daughter!

Besides, he wasn't a man to overlook a crime. Raised by a father who was a judge, he'd spent his entire life working for and within the law for the public interest. His finely honed sense of justice demanded he get satisfaction from the situation, not only for himself, but for the people he might soon represent at a national level.

He wanted to know who and why... and he wanted to prosecute the guilty parties to the extent of the law.

"No police," he agreed tersely, "on one condition."

"What?"

"You'll have to prove yourself."

"Anything. I'll do anything," she promised.

"Good." Dakota said, though he didn't think she was going to like this one. "Because you're going to have to work with me to turn the tables on the kidnappers."

Chapter Two

"Work with you?" Honor didn't know why she was surprised. What else had she expected? That he would beg her not to try to steal his papers again? "But they're professionals."

"Then they won't suspect we're trying to trap them."

Honor wanted to scream at Dakota, but years of acting experience allowed her to keep her voice controlled. "The life of a four-year-old child is on the line here. If we make a mistake—"

"Then we won't make a mistake."

"You can afford to say that. Nora isn't your daughter. She's mine, and I'm terrified they'll harm her."

"There are no guarantees, not even if you give them what they want."

A lump settled in Honor's throat as she met blue eyes as brilliant as aquamarines. Recognizing the shadow of pity in them, she dropped her gaze and stared at the pronounced cleft in Dakota's chin.

She knew what he said was true and that she'd been trying to fool herself. She'd convinced herself that if she did exactly what the kidnappers said, Nora would be freed. But deep inside, Honor also knew that Nora could be a liability to criminals who didn't want to be identified. Perhaps she'd been stupid, but believing that God wouldn't be so cruel as to take her daughter from her permanently was the only thing that had gotten her through the past thirty-two hours.

Honor moved to the spot where Dakota had tackled her, where manila folders, papers and photographs had popped out of the hanging file and now lay strewn across the floor. She started to gather them.

"What do you propose?" she asked.

"To follow you. To stop the person who comes to pick up the ransom."

Her head whipped toward him. "You can't. If the others don't get these papers..."

Dakota took the documents from her. "You won't have these papers to give in the first place."

"What do you mean?" she demanded, fighting the panic that had threatened to envelope her since the unthinkable had happened. "I have to give the kidnappers what they want in trade for my daughter!"

"Or a reasonable facsimile thereof," Dakota argued. "I have a neutral report we had commissioned several months ago, before we really got into this case. You can have that. I can forge a couple of statements similar to but less incriminating than the real McCoys. And I have dozens of photographs of salmon boats that I can use, but which could be useful as subterfuge. Maybe whoever's behind the kidnapping can be lulled into thinking we don't have anything of importance," he said, more to himself than to her.

"Why even bother having me deliver anything if you're going to stop the pick-up man?" she asked bitterly.

How could any decent person be so callous when a child's safety might be on the line? she wondered.

"The pick-up man could get away. Or I could follow him," he conceded. "That might be better, anyway. Where are you supposed to meet the guy?"

Honor thought quickly. "Pike Place Market." She'd be damned if she'd tell him the truth if there was any chance she could get away from him and make the real drop. "And I'm not supposed to meet anyone. I was told to leave the files behind one of the stalls."

She tried not to look too relieved when he nodded, obviously swallowing her story. Though she would have to make due with whatever he was willing to let her take, she could hope it would be enough for the kidnappers—or that it would at least buy her some time. Now all she had to do was figure out how to get away from Dakota so she could appear at the real rendezvous site alone, as instructed.

Putting the office right and preparing the fake documents took nearly an hour, time enough for Honor to conceive of a plan to counter the one Dakota formulated. As they left the office, she picked up the envelope and tucked it into her side. Dakota didn't argue, though he kept an eye on her as she accompanied him docilely to the elevator.

As he pressed the call button, she moved away, saying, "I'll be right back."

Dakota grabbed her free wrist. "You're not going anywhere without me."

"Fine. Come to the ladies lounge with me, then, but I can't leave until I make a stop." She gave him a pained expression. "You know what nerves can do—"

"All right. Let's go."

Honor hurried around the corner, Dakota on her heels. She prayed he'd been raised with too much class to actually follow her inside. The elevator was already creaking and groaning its way up to the fifth floor. She had only a minute or so to execute her plan with the aid of the noisy old contraption to cover her movements.

"Hurry," he said, stopping at the door.

She flashed him a smile of real gratitude—she was almost sorry she had to dupe him this way—slipped inside the lounge, and, the second the door closed, went for her tote bag into which she placed the envelope. Her heart was pounding and she could hear the elevator grinding to a halt as she ran on tiptoe and exited through the door into the other hallway. Without hesitating, she moved quickly but quietly toward the fire-stairs exit she'd spotted earlier. Now, if only she could get down to street level before Dakota caught up to her.

Taking the stairs two at a time, Honor pulled a calf-length red-knit duster from the bag and slipped it on. Fourth floor. She pulled out a dark curly wig and fought to get her braid under it as she kept moving. Third. A pair of horned-rimmed glasses came next. Second. Bright red lipstick. When she got to the first floor, she stopped a second to slip into a different pair of shoes.

About to open the door, she hesitated. The guard might be suspicious that she'd used the stairs instead of the elevator. A few seconds delay and Dakota could catch up to her. So she kept going, descending deeper into the bowels of the building—a poorly lit basement that seemed to be a maze of pipes and obstacles. A mistake, or so she thought until she spotted the loading dock doors. Making an instant decision, she crossed the basement and burst through the door, setting off an alarm.

She hit the sidewalk at a run and immediately headed for her car, which she'd left more than a block away. Although it was almost ten, people moved along the streets. Few bothered to look her way. Many were homeless. None posed a threat.

Out of breath by the time she got to her car, she climbed in and waited only until her pulse steadied before starting the ignition. Dakota Raferty would be cursing her by now. He was probably calling the police. They wouldn't find her, not until she'd made the delivery. And once she had her daughter in her arms safe and sound, she didn't care what threats they used against her.

She could afford the best lawyers, Honor told herself, thinking positively about Nora's return. Her actions had been justified. Any reasonable person could understand that.

But in case they didn't, maybe she would take her daughter and disappear off the face of the earth.

As Honor sped to the docks at the south end of Elliott Bay, her only regret was that she'd had to betray a friend. Sydney Raferty didn't deserve this from her.

And neither, she suspected, fighting a rush of guilt, did Sydney's brother.

DAKOTA CALLED HIMSELF every kind of fool as the elevator touched down on the first floor and the alarm went off. He'd been suckered by a clever woman—again—and he didn't like being played for a fool one bit.

As the doors opened, he saw the night guard leaving his post, gun in hand.

"Grady—"

"Not now, Mr. Raferty. Sorry, but I gotta check out the alarm!"

Dakota could have told the guard that he was too late, that someone had been leaving the building rather than breaking in. Instead of taking the time to stop the guy and explain, however, Dakota raced out the front exit, around the corner and toward the loading dock area. As he'd suspected, he didn't get a glimpse of Honor Bright, who was a better actress than he could have imagined.

He'd actually believed her. . . .

Knowing he was being even more of a fool, he headed for his car and Pike Place Market.

As he'd known it would be, the market was locked up but for the few restaurants with late hours. And he saw no sign of a stunning redhead. Furious that not only had she given him the slip but had lied about the drop-off location, as well, Dakota thought to call the police.

But what if she'd been telling the truth about her daughter?

He couldn't get the possibility out of his mind. No matter that he thought Honor should have gone to the police herself, he couldn't do it. When he found a telephone, he dialed the number Sydney had given him a few days before. He couldn't believe she was spending her nights reading Tarot cards in a bar.

"Benno's place," came a familiar voice raised over the sounds of laughter and music.

"Syd?"

"Dakota? How's it going?" Sydney asked. Then anxiously she said, "Is anything wrong?"

"No," he hurried to assure her.

He didn't want Sydney tied up in knots with his problems, not after what she'd been through. The victim of a con man out to even an old score, she'd been gaslighted by a supposedly new husband who had then supposedly died—neither case having been true—in addition to which, she'd been suspected of murder and had almost perished in a fire. The past month had been a living hell for her.

"So what's up?" Sydney asked.

"I met your friend Honor Bright this evening."

"Ah-ha!"

"What's the 'ah-ha' for?"

"I'm not naive, brother dear. I know your taste in women. Your hormones are stirred up and you're obsessed, right?"

Not about to tell his sister what he really thought of the actress—though obsession might not be totally inaccurate—Dakota hedged. "That Honor is a real beauty, all right. Smart, too."

He couldn't believe how stupid he'd felt when he'd remembered the second door to the ladies' lounge. He'd stormed into the room only to find her gone.

"And she's been divorced for more than a year."

He recognized Sydney's matchmaking tone and played on the fact to get the information he sought. "Must be tough raising a kid all alone."

"I know for a fact that Honor considers raising Nora a joy rather than some tough duty divorce forced on her," Sydney assured him.

So Honor did have a daughter—at least that much hadn't been a lie.

"She took the job in Seattle because of her daughter, you know," his sister continued. "Honor wanted a quieter life for a while so she could spend more time with Nora and make a home where her little girl would have some stability for once. Traipsing around to various shooting locations can be pretty tough on a four-year-old."

So could kidnapping. Dakota suspected little Nora had had that carefully manufactured security ripped away from her, just as her mother had claimed. Still nothing could excuse Honor's illegal actions. Even if he hesitated to bring in the police, he wasn't about to let her perfidy go as if it had never happened. Especially not when he was the target of the real criminals who might strike at his campaign in some other manner if they weren't satisfied with their end of the deal.

Now all he had to do was find Honor with his unsuspecting sister's help—help that Honor would no doubt be expecting.

"Speaking of home—you wouldn't have Honor's telephone number and address, would you?"

"What? You didn't get them?" Sydney laughed. "My big brother is slipping in his old age. I remember a time when a woman would force that information on you whether or not you wanted it."

"We didn't exactly have the opportunity," Dakota said dryly. Not to mention the incentive. "Come on, Syd, stop ragging on me and find your address book."

"I don't have to. I know the address by heart. Got a pencil?"

"And my trusty black book."

In which he scribbled the address Sydney gave him. "That's the Capitol Hill area."

"Across from Volunteer Park. Hey, want me to call Honor and put in the good word for you?"

"No!" he said quickly. "Don't you dare try to help me. Besides, I think she got a definite first impression of me that she won't soon forget."

Sydney chuckled. "Bigheaded as always. One of these days, a woman is going to knock the stuffing out of you, Prince Charming."

"One already did." He'd never forget his ex-fiancée, Maureen O'Neil, who had been as deceptive as they'd come. "I don't plan on letting it happen again."

"Love finds us whether or not we're ready for it," Sydney warned him with a dreamy sigh.

Knowing his sister thought she was in love with some character named Benno DeMartino just because the man saved her life, Dakota didn't argue. She couldn't have fallen for real, not so soon after the fiasco prompted by the late, shady Al Fox, a man she'd also thought she loved! The current romance would undoubtedly cool off as soon as Sydney came to her senses, but there was no need to upset her with that projection.

Bringing the conversation to a close with his promise to give their father Sydney's love, Dakota replaced the receiver and returned his notebook to his inside jacket pocket.

Honor's address was burned into his memory anyway, Dakota thought as he returned to his car. He was going to find the place and sit on her doorstep until the actress returned from her rendezvous, even if it meant waiting all night.

HONOR PARKED HER CAR in an all-but-deserted area under the viaduct along Alaskan Way. Now that she was about to make the drop, her adrenaline was rushing as fast as the vehicular traffic would on a good night.

This wasn't a good night for her, Honor thought, not unless Nora ended up in her arms because of it.

"Please, God, keep my little girl safe," she whispered. "Bring her home to me by morning."

They hadn't said when Nora would be returned. No promises until she delivered the goods.

What they *had* said was "before midnight."

She was early, a little after eleven. Ironic, considering she might not have been able to show at all. What they might have done to Nora if she hadn't come through was something she didn't want to contemplate. Uneasily, she fingered the envelope with its innocuous documents. If they thought she was trying to pull one over on them...

Unable to stand the wait any longer, she chose to act immediately and damn the early hour. By the time she crossed to the pier and dropped off the package, it would be almost eleven-thirty. Then she could get the hell out of there...or wait to see who made the pick up.

Her pulse ticked unevenly as she considered the daring notion, then tried to forget about it. Damn Dakota for giving her the idea in the first place.

Too dangerous, she told herself, not only for her, but for her daughter.

But not if she were the first to arrive and then found a safe place to hide, a little voice contradicted.

She wouldn't do anything foolish, Honor assured herself, carrying on with the fantasy. She wouldn't try to follow the man. She would merely watch. Observe.

Maybe she would notice something that would identify the kidnapper later when she could finally report the crime to the police.

What was she thinking of? Hadn't she decided to take her daughter and disappear so no one could ever threaten Nora again? No, Honor admitted to herself, she hadn't decided anything of the kind. Not for certain. She wasn't a coward, and running from anything or anyone went against her grain. Taking Nora from the first real home they'd shared for more than a few months at a time would be cruel.

Besides, she didn't have Nora yet.

First things first.

Choosing to wear the wig and fake glasses in case anyone saw her, she shed the red duster. It was too conspicuous and she wanted to blend into her surroundings as best she could. Before getting out of the car, she took a thorough look around. No other human traffic in sight.

Nerves tingling, she slid out into the dark night, envelope tucked tightly under one arm.

Her eyes kept moving, watching, observing only a few other cars parked in the area, most notably a souped up Olds with tires too large for its frame, a Plymouth with a vanity license plate reading HOTSHOT, and a silver BMW of indeterminate age. She kept watch for their possible owners, but neither saw nor heard anyone as she crossed to the dock area.

Her heart was in her throat as she strode forward, her sense of unreality growing by leaps and bounds. She felt as though her body didn't exactly belong to her. Someone else was moving the legs that closed the distance to the wharf. Another pressed the arm that held the precious package at her side. Even the ache that started in the pit of her stomach and spread to her extremities seemed once removed, sort of like a toothache more remembered than felt.

As she drew closer to the drop-off site, she began to understand the real meaning of fear, which skulked through her chest and slithered around her lungs until she felt as if she would suffocate.

The setting was so ominous.

Unlike the brightly lit, noisy piers just a short distance to the north, this one wasn't in use. It was deserted. Eerily quiet. Dark.

Dangerous.

The night was moonless, the stars swallowed by the cloud cover overhead. Black. Everything was so black. Only a few lights washed pale pools of silver-blue over small areas of the dock and its ramshackle warehouses. Mist crawled up from the ocean, writhing and twisting along the wooden planking now beneath her feet, circling her ankles like prison chains that slowed her down.

Feeling all too vulnerable, Honor had the distinct sensation that she was being watched.

Quickly looking over her shoulder toward the first building she'd passed, she saw no one. Her gaze then skimmed the larger hulking warehouse that squatted before her on the pier. No light, no movement, no indication of another human presence. Ears attuned for the slightest sound, she relaxed a bit when all she heard were waves lapping against the pilings below.

She was imagining things, Honor told herself, trying to make light of the spooky sensation. Undoubtedly, she wouldn't feel safe for a long time after this incident was over. The distinct, familiar smell of the ocean assaulted her nose and she reveled in the sharp scent of reality, a combination of salt and fish.

Fish.

That reminded her of salmon, her reason for being here—her daughter in trade for some stupid documents that could point a wagging finger at the salmon-fishing industry.

It just didn't make sense that someone wanting such information would go to these extreme lengths to get it. Why involve an innocent person, an outsider? she wondered. Unless there was more to the mystery than she'd suspected. She hadn't thought with a clear mind since Nora had been snatched, and now wasn't the time to indulge herself.

Later, she promised herself. After Nora was safe, Honor would help Dakota any way she could. She owed him that.

But now she was going to deliver the documents as instructed.

She forced her legs to move, counted doorways, found the old supply box at the fifth mooring down. With one last quick look around to assure herself she had no witnesses—though the sensation of being watched still clung to her subconscious—she slid the envelope inside. And then she retreated, her steps quick and sure as though the only thought on her mind was to get out of there.

Exactly what she should have done.

But when she passed the smaller warehouse nearest the street, she melded with its shadows and swung behind a staircase that she could use as cover. She hadn't known she was going to do so until that very second.

She'd thought she was going to be smart, watch out for herself and Nora.

That's exactly what she was doing, Honor realized. Dakota had been right. She couldn't count on the word of a criminal, and she was desperate to find her daughter.

Not knowing what her next move would be, she sat on a discarded fruit crate and waited.

She couldn't shake the certainty that someone else nearby waited, as well.

The luminous dials of her watch warned her as midnight approached. Rather than revving up as she might expect, her nerves calmed, leaving behind cold anger that cleared her mind and honed her senses.

A scrabbling sound behind her whipped Honor off her seat. She spotted a wharf rat poking around, probably looking for food. Her heart pounded.

In the distance, a church bell tolled.

Midnight.

The magic hour.

To her relief, the rat scurried away, freeing her attention, and just in time. Someone was moving cautiously along the other warehouse, nearing the drop-off site. No wonder she'd felt as if she were being watched! The pick-up man had beat her to the site and had been lying in wait.

Whoever it was would have to come past her to get away, however, and when he did . . .

Honor peeked out further from behind the staircase as a paper rustled behind her. The rat had returned. She steeled herself against being distracted. A dark form was sneaking out from the warehouse shadows, entering a pool of silver-blue light. As though suspecting she was watching, the person turned to stare in her direction.

Honor ducked back into her own shadows and counted to ten before daring to stick out her head once more. Startled, she saw no one. But she hadn't given the person enough time to retrieve the documents and get away! What was going on?

About to take yet another step from her hiding place, Honor heard a noise behind her too loud and distinct to be made by a rat. Before she could turn to face her danger, pain exploded through the back of her head, her vision blurred and stars lit her inner sky.

And then the brightness faded to twilight....

Chapter Three

Awareness gradually permeated the black void holding Honor captive.

Awareness and excruciating pain.

Despite the agony searing her head, she opened her eyes and blinked in confusion until she remembered where she was and why. A broken reminder lay inches from her nose—the glasses she'd worn as part of her disguise. She could barely make out the bent frames and shattered lenses in the early-morning light.

Dawn was beginning to spread its gray misery over Seattle. Rain drizzled steadily, forming puddles along the dock. The smell of fish was so overwhelming that her stomach clutched in response. She swallowed hard to still the convulsions. Shivering from the cold damp and a crawly sensation between her shoulder blades, she tried to push herself up into a sitting position.

An angry squeak and the scrabbling of tiny claws down her spine terrorized her into temporary paralysis.

"Aaahh!"

The rodent went flying. Honor jerked upright to her feet then caught on to the staircase to steady herself as her stomach threatened to empty. Everything was spinning, and her head felt as big as Mount Rainier.

"I'm going, lady. Don't make no more fuss."

"What?"

She jumped yet again at the unexpected voice. Pain vibrated from her scalp to her toes and she had trouble focusing as she turned to see a man dressed in rags scrambling out from under a blanket of newspapers a few yards away. He'd obviously taken shelter from the rain under the overhang.

"Please. I didn't mean no harm, lady," the transient assured her.

He scurried away as quickly as the rat had done.

Honor stared after the man, her heart saddened. Seattle had more than its share of homeless, no doubt due less to unemployment than to the mild year-round climate that drew transients from other states. The poor man had undoubtedly thought she was reacting to him. He was probably more frightened than she.

And she *was* frightened, Honor realized, not because of the rat, not because of the homeless man, but because of the damage her foolishness might have wreaked.

Despair enveloped her as she realized what she'd done. Damn Dakota Raferty for putting the idea in her head! She shouldn't have tried to outwit the criminals. She should have followed orders and gone home to wait. Even now, Nora might be safe and warm, snug in her arms.

Who knew how the criminal mind worked?

Who knew how the kidnappers might punish Honor for disobeying them?

Then, again, maybe she was blowing things out of proportion. Maybe they thought they had what they wanted. Maybe they had returned her daughter, Honor thought hopefully, or left a message on her machine regarding Nora's whereabouts.

Only one way to find out.

She took a tentative step. Her toe connected with something solid, almost tripping her. She looked down at a length of steel pipe—probably the weapon used to knock her out—but she moved her head too quickly. Nausea overwhelmed her.

Hanging on to the staircase, she bent over, took a deep whiff of the ocean and let the fishy smell do its worst.

When her stomach was empty, she wiped her sleeve across her mouth and waited until she was able to draw in air without her stomach and chest heaving. Then she pushed herself away from the warehouse and stumbled out from under her shelter. Neither a downpour nor a mist, the rain was heavy enough to permeate her clothing before she reached Alaskan Way. Few vehicles were on the road this early, but a ferry at the next pier was getting ready to depart.

Still woozy, she waited until her footing firmed, then weaved toward her car, which stood alone under the viaduct. She was soaked to the skin and shaking before she found her keys and got inside. Her head bobbled back against the head rest, and her eyelids fluttered closed.

Sleep tempted her.

Until she remembered Nora.

She started the ignition. The engine shuddered its complaint against the dampness, but the car moved off without dying. Carefully, she turned into the light dawn traffic and somehow, miraculously, found her way across the downtown area to Capitol Hill without having an accident. Rather than fighting with the garage, she pulled up in front of the house and parked at the curb.

As Honor exited the car, her Queen Anne-style home looked as stately and beautiful as always, but this morning, it was anything but inviting. Not that she was really surprised.

There on her wrap-around, flower-bedecked porch, sprawled across the long rattan swing, Dakota Raferty lay in wait for her.

"FINALLY." DAKOTA SHIFTED into a sitting position and stretched. Narrowing his gaze, he focused on the ridiculous wig Honor was wearing. Part of some stupid disguise. She'd been in too many movies. He kept his voice deceptively calm as he asked, "Have a satisfactory night on the town?"

Honor tried to rush past him, but she was moving as if she were drunk. Before she got to the door, he easily grabbed her arm, effectively stopping her. She swayed and caught his jacket lapel to steady herself. Her full breasts pressed against his chest, but she didn't seem to notice. She was stumbling with exhaustion. That her face appeared pale and pinched in the gray dawn didn't escape his notice.

"Satisfied?" he probed when she remained tight-lipped and hostile.

"I did what I had to for my daughter."

"So where is she? I don't see her with you."

She shoved at his chest ineffectually. "Let go of me...."

"Or you'll what?" he challenged.

He thought she was about to cry, then he realized her eyes seemed strangely glazed, as if she were unable to focus properly. When she pushed at him again, he let go of her, though he had no intention of letting her escape him this time, not until he had some answers and assurances.

If he could trust her to be honest about either. He expected more of someone named Honor than she was likely to give.

Her hand shook as she tried to unlock the door. Dakota took over. When he got the door open, he held it for her in a gentlemanly gesture she surely didn't appreciate. She wandered into the room as if it were a strange place rather than her home. Acting dazed, she looked around, then weaved toward a telephone and answering machine.

"They didn't call!" she cried in frustration as she got halfway there. "Maybe she's upstairs. Nora! Nora, honey, are you here?"

An emotion Dakota couldn't quite identify twisted his gut as he recognized the agony in her voice. He'd told her there were no guarantees. He reached out to her with more gentleness than she deserved. For the first time, he realized she was soaked to the skin and shivering. He turned her to face him and was once more struck by the dullness of her eyes.

"She's not here, Honor."

"I know."

The words escaped her lips in a soft rush. She swayed and might have fallen if he hadn't wrapped an arm around her back to steady her. This wasn't the same woman who'd fought him like a wildcat the night before.

"Are you all right?" he asked as he helped her to a sofa and made her sit.

Her hands went to her head. "If only it would stop."

"What?"

"The pounding. Someone hit me...with a pipe, I think."

"Good God, why didn't you say so." He kneeled and took off the wig, heard her sigh of relief at the release of such slight pressure. "How long ago did this happen?"

"I don't know exactly. I remember hearing a church bell at midnight. The next thing I knew, it was dawn."

"You were unconscious for that many hours?" No wonder her eyes looked so strange. "We have to get you to an emergency room."

"No! I can't leave. They'll call about Nora. I know they will."

"And what do you think you're going to accomplish by running around with a concussion? You drove like this. You could have killed yourself...or someone else. You have to get medical help and then talk to the police."

She pressed her eyelids closed, but tears seeped through them. "No emergency room, no police!" she cried softly. "Involving anyone official might sign Nora's death warrant." Her green eyes, open once more, pleaded with him when she asked, "Could you live with yourself if something happened to her because of you?"

"All right, no police for now, and no emergency room. Maybe a doctor—"

"I can't leave!"

And neither could he, Dakota realized. He was stuck with Honor, at least temporarily. Someone had to take care of her.

"Where were you hit?"

She indicated the area and he carefully checked her scalp. She had a doozer of a lump and a small area of broken skin. No doubt the stupid wig had acted as a cushion, saving her from greater injury.

"You're lucky whoever did this didn't split open your skull. Do you have some kind of painkiller in the house?"

"Extra-strength aspirins." She was obviously relieved that he wasn't going to force outside help on her. "In the upstairs medicine cabinet."

Dakota gave her a long, penetrating look, but he didn't think she was acting this time. "Stay put."

She leaned against the couch and moaned.

He rushed up the stairs and tore into the bathroom. He found not only aspirins on the highest shelf of the medicine cabinet, but hydrogen peroxide, as well. Then he hunted up some gauze swabs and poured water into a paper cup. As he was leaving, a thick dark green bathrobe caught his eye and he grabbed it, too.

When he returned to the first floor, Honor was still cushioned by the couch, eyes closed.

"Hey, are you awake?" he asked.

"Uh-huh."

He gave her the aspirin first, then took care of the scalp wound. Though he was as gentle as he knew how to be, he hurt her. Not that she complained. He could tell by the way she stiffened and sucked in her breath.

"You're going to have to get out of those wet clothes and into this," he said, indicating the robe.

Her eyes widened slightly and he thought she was about to argue. Dakota turned to give her the privacy she needed. He closed his mind to what she might look like beneath the loose olive top.

But when she groaned and murmured, "I can't," he knew he had to help her.

Her arms were tangled in the loose garment, which she'd slipped up to her neck. She was attempting to get it over her head. And with each try, she was bringing herself more misery.

Dakota did his best to ignore her breasts, which were all but spilling out of flesh-colored lace cups as he helped free her from the garment. Nevertheless, a spark of awareness passed through him that he hoped she wouldn't recognize. He was a healthy male with normal appetites, but he didn't think being faced with that knowledge would make her comfortable under the current conditions.

"Thanks," she murmured, quickly grabbing the robe to cover herself.

He turned his back but was acutely aware of her movements. The brush of material. The snap of the bra. Spandex sliding over her lush hips and down her long, long legs. The images the sounds conjured made him hard and uncomfortable. He derided himself for being so weak, for being physically attracted to a woman who had perpetrated a criminal act against him, but he couldn't help himself any more than he could help pitying her for what she was going through.

"Ooh, that's better," Honor said, chasing a shudder. "I hadn't realized how cold I was."

Dakota faced her. The robe was wrapped tightly across her unbound breasts, and her fingers clutched the plush collar to her long, elegant neck. She looked so innocent... and so vulnerable.

The innocent part was a facade, as he well knew. He only hoped he wasn't being taken in by the other.

"Thank you," she said softly, the two words holding a wealth of meaning.

Taking a step closer, Dakota tilted her chin and looked into her eyes. He'd only meant to ascertain whether or not she had a concussion—both pupils seemed equally dilated—but he became trapped by the wealth of emotion he found in them. Pain. Guilt. Gratitude.

"Why don't you lie down?" he suggested, removing his hand.

"I might fall asleep."

Exhaustion was consuming her. He could see it in the droop of her flawless features, hear it in the slur of her dulcet tones. Dakota suspected she would drift off the moment her head touched down.

"You won't be any good to anyone like this."

Her gaze slid to the telephone. "But if they call—"

"I'll wake you."

She studied him for a moment. "Why?"

"Because I'll be here."

"That's not what I mean. Why will you be here? Why are you helping me when I..." Her voice dropped off along with her gaze.

"I don't know why. Maybe because I feel sorry for you. For your loss," he amended.

She stiffened. "Nora is not lost to me!"

"I didn't say she was."

"Don't even think it." Her voice hardened, bright spots of color emerged at the crest of her cheekbones, and her eyes glittered like twin emeralds. "I'm going to get my daughter back, no matter what I have to do."

Dakota believed it. That was the problem. He had trouble with shades of gray when it came to the law. Always had. As far as he was concerned, a crime was a crime... and she'd committed one. But all he said was, "In the meantime, get some rest."

She seemed uncertain, but in the end, exhaustion— not only of the body but of the spirit, Dakota decided—won. She lay curled on her side with her knees to her chest. Her body trembled, and she wrapped her arms closely around her, as if seeking more warmth.

Dakota spotted an afghan, a bright flood of colors folded and hung on the back of a rocking chair near the fireplace. He retrieved the covering and laid it over her. She murmured her thanks as her eyelids fluttered, then settled against her pale skin.

He moved to the window and stared out at the rain, every so often glancing her way to make sure she was all right. Her breathing grew deep within moments.

Quietly pacing, he took in the room, which was as comfortable as the afghan. This certainly was no Hollywood showplace as he might have expected. The furnishings were expensive, but they didn't put one off. A plain, comfortable, tan sofa and cinnamon chairs. A Turkish rug whose intricate design pulled the room together. Antique woods, restored and highly polished.

He noticed a toy on an end table—a soft purple dragon just the right size to be squeezed by a small hand.

And photographs lined the fireplace mantel, mostly of a copper-braided little girl doing silly little girl things, yet all framed beautifully as if they were prized possessions. Only one was a formal portrait.

Dakota studied the picture of mother and daughter, so alike in coloring and expression. The same impishness on Nora's face was reflected in Honor's. He'd never seen her looking like this in movies or commercials. A beauty that came from happiness found deep within shone over her famous face.

He glanced toward the couch where the flesh-and-blood woman was becoming restless. She was frowning and making low noises as if she were crying in her sleep.

He could hardly believe this Honor Bright was the same carefree, vivacious woman as the one in the picture on the mantel.

Responding to her instinctively, Dakota crossed to the couch, ran the back of his fingers over Honor's cheek and smoothed a loose strand of copper hair. His touch must have soothed her, for after a moment, she quieted and her breathing grew deeper. Disturbed by the effect she was having on him, he chose to sit in the rocking chair a safe distance away, his attention split between the lace underwear tossed on the floor, the gloom of the rainy morning outside the windows and the woman on the couch.

She didn't look like a criminal.

That's what he couldn't get out of his head. He glanced at the portrait on the mantel and wondered what he would have done if he had been in her position, if Nora had been his daughter.

But, of course, he couldn't imagine it. Though he was thirty-six-years-old, he had no children. No wife. No desire to make a commitment to another woman after the way Maureen had betrayed him. He was best in easy relationships, ones with surface passion and no strings. He saved his real inner fire for his work, for the betterment of humanity.

But what was humanity if not millions of individuals like Honor and Nora?

Before he had to face the question squarely, the shrill of the telephone startled him. He vaulted up to answer it, even as Honor's eyes blinked open and she struggled to rise.

"Nora," she whispered.

Something in him inexplicably responded to the mixture of terror and hope he heard in that single word, and he knew exactly what he would have done had he been in her position.

SLEEP-CLUMSY, HONOR COULDN'T get to the telephone quick enough. Her feet seemed to trip her as she led the way, Dakota on her heels.

"Please, God, let them be fooled," she mumbled, shaking off the last of her grogginess. "Please let them tell me where to find Nora."

She picked up the receiver halfway through the third ring, just before the answering machine clicked on. Meeting Dakota's encouraging gaze, she tried to keep her voice normal.

"Hello."

Her voice was normal maybe, but not much else. Her heart was pounding wildly, pulsing blood to her extremities at a too-rapid pace.

"Hiya, babe, didn't wake you, did I?"

Honor steadied herself against the table when she realized it was only Gary. "Uh, yes, as a matter of fact, you did." Not a lie. Definitely a disappointment. Groping for something to say, she asked, "What time is it?"

"Almost seven-thirty. You catching up on your beauty sleep?"

"Something like that."

To Dakota, she shook her head and mouthed, "Ex-husband."

"As if you needed it," Gary said in a tone she recognized. He wanted something, but she didn't know what. She didn't care to know. She was through with Gary's demands and pleas, had been since she'd left L.A.

"I just got home from location last night," Gary continued in the self-important tone she'd learned to hate. "Damn, shooting *Desert Barbarians* was grueling...."

Gary went on about his current film until Honor wanted to scream at him to get off the phone so the kidnappers could get through to her. But, of course, he didn't know about the situation, and she had no intention of telling him.

"...But you know how that goes," Gary was saying.

"Right," Honor agreed, though she hadn't the faintest notion to what. Unable to concentrate on anything but Nora, she shrugged helplessly at Dakota, who by now was leaning against the back of the couch. "Listen, this isn't a good time for me. I forgot to set my alarm and I'm late," she lied. "I've got to jump in the shower right now."

"Remember how we used to shower together, babe?"

"I remember too many things to romanticize our marriage, Gary," she snapped. "Listen, I really have to hurry."

"Wait a minute!" he insisted. "I want to say hi to my pumpkinhead."

"You can't."

"Why not?"

"Because Nora's not here."

Panicked at what kind of an excuse to use, she signaled to Dakota for help. Pantomiming, he folded his hands together and lay his head on them like a pillow.

So when Gary asked, "Where is she?" Honor responded, "Sleeping."

"You mean she doesn't wake you up at sunrise anymore?"

He'd bought it. She sagged with relief. "Sometimes, but last night, she stayed up past her bedtime."

"Well, give her a smooch from her old dad and tell her I'll call her later."

"Sure, I'll do that. Bye, Gary."

She slammed the receiver into its cradle and leaned on it, not believing for a moment that he would actually follow through. Dakota was staring at her, waiting. No doubt he wanted an explanation.

"Gary would just screw things up if I told him."

"If he's Nora's father, he has rights, don't you think?"

"He gave up his rights a long time ago."

"Because he divorced you?"

"No, I divorced Gary Webster for a number of reasons—blondes, brunettes, redheads. And he couldn't be a real father to Nora any more than he could be faithful to me."

"I'm sorry. But he must love his daughter."

"Oh, now and then, when he remembers he has one. After the separation, he only saw her when I was around. An excuse to see me. As ridiculously unfaithful as he was, I guess he still loved me in a sick way. But Nora?" She shook her head sadly. "He didn't fight for custody until I took the job here. Then it was only to stop me from moving permanently out of his life. He couldn't believe he lost."

"Sounds like it would be tough on the kid."

"You have no idea. Nora loves her daddy. But since we moved here from L.A., Gary missed both her fourth birthday and Christmas. His presents were weeks late, obviously picked up in a hurry without any thought. He couldn't even remember to call. So why did he now?"

"Maybe he sensed something was wrong."

A horrible thought struck Honor. But, no, not even Gary was that malicious. Or was he? Her mind reeled with the ugly possibility.

"Honor, what is it?"

She stared into Dakota's aquamarine eyes. "More than once, Gary told me I'd never be rid of him, that he would always have a hold on me through our daughter. Good God, what if Gary stole Nora to get back at me for leaving L.A.?"

Chapter Four

"Your ex-husband's being involved doesn't make sense," Dakota stated.

"Nothing Gary does makes sense."

Honor moved away from the telephone, circled the couch and stopped in front of the windows. Hugging herself, she stared across the street at the park, a green jewel only slightly dulled by the gray skies. She couldn't count the hours she'd spent with Nora in that setting. The memory sank her deeper in depression. At least the rain had let up, she noted absently—not that the fact would improve her mood.

"Do you seriously think your ex-husband is so consumed with fury at your leaving that he'd mastermind some complex plot to get back at you?" Dakota asked.

"I don't know." Put that way, she had to admit it didn't sound like Gary, who usually reacted to things in a more immediate, unpleasant manner. "He is a self-involved, selfishly motivated poor excuse for a human being."

"With that kind of recommendation, why did you marry him in the first place?"

"Despite the B movies he normally stars in," she said, turning to face Dakota, "Gary Webster is a *very* good actor. He had me fooled until it was too late."

Dakota nodded as if he could empathize, and again it registered on her that he was a really outstanding looking man, as different from her ex-husband as day was from night, if equally compelling. His ash-blond hair was crisply styled, framing a face that was so perfectly male, it almost seemed sculpted—broad forehead, slanted cheekbones and sensual lips added to the deep cleft in his chin.

"So, if your ex-husband is obsessed with you, why would he try to make you do something criminal?" Dakota prodded. "And why against my lobbying efforts? How would he even know about me or about the issues?"

Honor sighed. "I don't know." He was making more sense of the situation than she. "But then, I don't seem to know much about anything anymore." She rubbed her temples, willing away the dull ache that threaded through her skull. "Maybe if I could actually get some sleep, I could figure things out."

"How's the head?"

"Better, if not great. At least I remember I have a meeting at NCSC this morning. We're supposed to be discussing some personal appearances. Now all I have to do is stay awake long enough to call with some excuse—"

"No," Dakota interrupted, "you'll have to go."

She stared at him. "Don't be ridiculous. My first concern is my daughter."

"That's why you have to follow through with your schedule. You don't want anyone to suspect anything unusual is going on. You're a damn good actress. You can keep up a pretense so that everything seems normal."

Annoyance at his dictatorial manner made her snap, "And I can call in and say I'm sick, for heaven's sake."

"And another thing," Dakota went on, ignoring the flash of temper, "something you might not have considered. Maybe someone at the council is involved."

"What?"

"That never occurred to you?" Sounding incredulous, he now was doing the staring. "Think about it. The papers you were supposed to steal had incriminating information about several companies in the salmon-fishing industry. And who represents these companies?"

Honor blinked. "I guess I do, as spokesperson for the Northwest Coast Salmon Council."

"Of which I am a sometimes opponent through my lobbying efforts on behalf of environmentalists. Someone pitted us against each other. Irony? Or careful planning?"

"I didn't even think things through," she admitted. "I was so worried about Nora I just acted. I didn't take the time to analyze anything. I feel so stupid!"

"Don't. Just go to that meeting and keep your eyes and your ears open."

HONOR REMEMBERED DAKOTA'S admonition as she entered the office of Willard Zahniser, CEO of the Northwest Coast Salmon Council, a few minutes before ten.

The executive sat behind his desk, signing a stack of documents. In his midfifties, Zahniser was balding and portly, and wore thick glasses that distorted the shape of his gray eyes, making it impossible to read what lurked behind them. His appearance was that of the little man, but his exterior had never fooled Honor. Zahniser was a dynamic individual, polished despite his sometimes gruff manner. He could put himself on an equal footing with company owners or fisherman at will.

She thought him capable of anything.

But kidnapping a child and using her as a pawn to win a power struggle in the legislature?

"Sit."

Without looking up, he indicated the conference table near the windows. She was taking her place when the other executives entered—three men and a woman. Zahniser didn't seem to notice that everyone had arrived, but Honor knew it was an act. He was a power broker and liked to make people wait just because he could.

The others were getting restless by the time the CEO finished with the stack of papers. Still, he took his time gathering his notebook, folder and pen. Before he could cross to the conference table, his door burst open with a bang and bounced against the wall.

His mild-looking features pulling into a formidable frown, Zahniser turned as Andrew Vaughn stalked into the office, his head enveloped in a haze of cigar smoke.

Honor had never liked the NCSC lobbyist. The man was a sleazeball, living proof of how low an individual could get to win an issue. He thought nothing of splattering mud on someone else if he could come out of the encounter on top. His appearance matched his performance. He was big boned and lanky, wore ill-fitting suits and unbelievably bad ties. Today's was a salmon screened on a wavy blue background, the kind of thing tourists bought in shops along the piers. He pulled his ever-present cigar from his mouth and looked down his beak of a nose at the shorter man.

"We gotta talk, Zahniser."

"I'm in conference."

"Now!" His beady eyes narrowed. "We can either step into the hall or air our dirty laundry in front of witnesses."

The two men glared at each other, and Honor was startled when the CEO gave way. "I'll only be a minute," he told the others as he followed Vaughn.

But the door he closed behind them wasn't thick enough to totally eradicate the raised voices. Honor strained to hear what they were saying. She caught something about fishing rights...

"...Illegal...Taking all the chances."

The lobbyist's statement slashed through Honor. Her heart began to pound.

Illegal? Chances? Kidnapping and blackmail?

She was thinking about making some excuse to get closer to the door when it banged open once more. Zahniser entered, his ferocious visage blurred by cigar smoke that Vaughn puffed into the room after him. The executive shut the door firmly on the lobbyist before turning to the now-silent group at the conference table.

His face transformed, a study in serenity.

"Now, let's get down to business," he said as if the last few minutes had never happened.

Honor stared at her employer. Willard Zahniser was as much a chameleon as any actor she knew. Vaughn was more forthright, a snake in snake's skin. So was

there a conspiracy? Vaughn taking orders from Zahniser?

Was her own employer ruthless enough to use her in
a game that could prove deadly to her daughter?

DAKOTA STEPPED OUT OF THE shower and rubbed himself down vigorously with a thick leaf-print towel that
added to the rainforest theme of his bathroom. Deep
green walls were hung with framed photos he'd taken
along the Hoh and Quinault on the Olympic Peninsula. Myriad moisture-loving plants crowded every
available ledge and foot of floor space.

Slinging the towel low over his hips, he made for the
telephone in the connecting loft bedroom. He probably should have placed the call the moment he walked
through the front door, but he'd wanted to get cleaned
up after he'd shed the clothes he'd slept in.

If one could call reclining on a moving porch swing
half the night sleep, Dakota thought as the connection
was made and he heard Reynard Stirling's deep voice.

"Stirling here."

"Reynard, it's Dakota."

"I was just thinking about you. How's our project
coming along?"

"That's what I wanted to talk to you about."

"Uh-oh. You sound tense. Andrew Vaughn getting
to you?"

"Vaughn always gets to me." Now there was a man
worthy of his suspicions. "But he's not why I'm calling—at least I'm not sure if he's involved."

"This isn't good news," Reynard stated matter-of-
factly.

"Nope. Actually, I was wondering if anything out of the ordinary has happened to you lately. More specifically, with your environmental interests."

For years, Reynard Stirling had been not only one of the richest men but *the* most visible environmentalist in the continental United States.

"Nothing unusual that I can think of," Reynard said, his words becoming more clipped with comprehension. "A few crank calls and letters. Typical annoyances. So what's been going on?"

"Someone is very interested in the salmon-fishing files."

"Who?"

"I could guess all day, but it would be pure speculation," Dakota admitted. "You tell anyone about the information you've been putting together?"

"I haven't been mouthing off, but there are always leaks. I trust my personal assistant implicitly, and I'm pretty sure about the PI I hired. Discretion is his business, and I pay him well for it. What about you?"

"The other lobbyists at the cooperative know we've been working together since common approval is policy, but they don't know the particulars."

"Not unless one of them got a look at your files. I assume *someone* did."

"Someone." Unwilling to reveal the situation—Nora wasn't his daughter, after all—Dakota hedged. "But I haven't lost anything, and the files will be safe as soon as I bring them home."

"Why do I have the feeling you're holding out on me?"

"I'd tell you if I could, Reynard."

A short silence was followed by the environmentalist saying, "I trust your judgment, Dakota. If I didn't, I wouldn't be trying to convince you to run for office. Have you given it any more thought?"

"How can I not think about running for the U.S. Senate when you're so persuasive?"

And Reynard was eager to back his campaign. Having worked on environmental issues together since Dakota's first year as a state congressman, the men made an effective team. And Reynard had pretty much convinced Dakota that while his lobbying efforts were important, he could do the most good working for the public interest at a national level.

They discussed the possibilities for a few minutes until Reynard had to go to a meeting.

"You let me know if anything unusual happens," Dakota told him. "And especially if someone shows an interest in the salmon-fishing activities."

"You'll be the first to know," Reynard assured him. "And, Dakota . . . be careful."

HONOR PARKED HER CAR and headed for the Pioneer Square address Dakota had given her. She was a half hour early. Zahniser had wound up the meeting in record time, and she hadn't felt like waiting at her house until it was time to meet Dakota.

She entered Pioneer Place Park, the heart of the district, whose handsome old brick and stone buildings from the 1890s had been renovated to house restaurants, theaters and shops. Dakota had told her he lived over a gallery in what had once been a low-rent artist's loft.

As she crossed the plaza, she noted a small group of children running across the open area in front of the wrought-iron-and-glass pergola. She averted her eyes and closed her ears to their raucous voices and shrill laughter. The reminder of her own loss was so painful that she could hardly stand being near them. Despite her attempt at distancing herself, a little girl with copper braids ran through her line of vision.

Honor's heart stopped for a moment and her feet stumbled over the cobblestones.

"Nora!" she cried as she darted forward and snatched the little girl's shoulder, spinning her around.

Large brown eyes widened in fright, and through a haze of disbelief, Honor heard shouting. Then the child was pulled from her grasp and Honor was faced with an angry adult.

"What do you think you're doing?" the woman screamed at her.

Blinking in confusion, Honor backed off. "I'm sorry. I made a mistake."

"I'll say you did. I should call the police!" the woman cried.

"No police," Honor whispered. "It was a mistake."

Feeling as if she were trying to escape a nightmare, Honor raced away from the growing knot of people.

"What was that all about?" a man asked.

"She tried to snatch my Amy!" the woman said.

Tried to snatch my Amy...!

Tried to snatch...!

The accusation rang in her ears as Honor found the correct address and staggered into the hallway. She was the one whose child had been snatched! She was the one who had a right to be angry! But all she felt was a cold numbness, an emptiness that ached. With the flat of her hand, she slapped at the bell marked Raferty over and over and prayed Dakota was home. She couldn't go back onto that street alone if her life depended on it.

A shrill buzz made her jump. Then the inner door opened and she was taking the wide, carved staircase to the third floor two steps at a time. As she approached the landing, the door on her right opened. Dakota stood there, clad only in a towel slung low on his hips.

"I'm early," she said faintly.

"And you look like hell."

He stepped back and she passed him, aware of his broad expanse of naked chest, yet strangely unaffected. She felt dazed, the way she had been when she'd left the Space Needle alone. Her feet took her into the middle of a large open area filled with sunlight and artist's renderings of mountain vistas. There she stopped and stared at one of the exquisite paintings rather than looking at Dakota.

"All right, what happened?" he asked, turning her to face him anyway.

"There was a little girl outside. A tiny redhead. I thought..."

"That she was Nora," he finished for her.

"Her mother accused me of trying to steal her away."

Honor dipped her head and swallowed hard. Her eyes burned, but they remained dry. She didn't think she had any tears left to shed.

"She couldn't know," Dakota said softly.

Before she realized what was happening, he had her folded in his arms. The warmth of his tanned chest pulsated through her, moving her in a strangely comforting way. The lightly muscled flesh beneath her fingertips was vibrant and inviting. The awareness made her distinctly uncomfortable and she pushed herself out of his grasp.

"I just need to sit down for a minute."

"And have a drink."

"No." She settled gingerly on the edge of the nearest of two pale gray couches and stared at the exquisite abstract area rug. "No drink. I need to be clearheaded."

But he ignored her and poured one anyway. He lifted her hand and wrapped it around the glass, pressing his fingers over hers as if he could pass on the life force that she so desperately needed to keep her going.

"Brandy. Take a sip. You'll feel better."

He loomed over her, seemingly ready to enforce his command. She took the sip to placate him. Fire shot down her throat into her twisted and cramped stomach. Within seconds, she began to relax from the inside out.

"Better?" he asked.

Nodding, she looked up at him. "Sorry. I usually have excellent control over my emotions. Comes from being an actress." Her fingers worried the glass in her hand. His expression was sympathetic and yet she sensed he was keeping a mental distance. "The incident was just so awful, so unreal—like being stuck in a nightmare that has me in its grip and won't let go."

"It will when we get your daughter back."

She gave him a grateful if tenuous smile. "I don't deserve your help."

"Maybe not, but neither did you deserve having Nora taken away from you. Just relax while I get dressed. Then we'll talk."

Dakota moved away from her, his long legs taking great strides toward the open staircase. She'd caught him at an awkward moment and amazingly enough, he didn't seem nearly as aware of it as she—though how he could not be in his state of undress, she didn't understand. Perhaps because he viewed her more as a problem to be solved than a woman. Even with all she had on her mind, she was aware of him on a more intimate level than she deemed appropriate.

As he ascended to the loft area, she couldn't tear her gaze from his muscular legs as powerful and seductively male as the rest of him.

Guilt flooded her and Honor looked down into her glass. She was somehow betraying Nora by allowing her thoughts to stray from her daughter's plight even for a moment. There was one thing she could do while she waited.

She called up to Dakota. "Do you mind if I use your telephone?"

"Go ahead."

A phone sat on an end table next to the couch. She dialed her own number and tapped in the code to check for messages on her answering machine.

Nothing.

Swallowing her disappointment along with another sip of brandy, Honor settled back on the couch. When would the kidnappers call? If she didn't hear soon, she would go out of her mind!

Trying to distract herself from the grim possibilities, she glanced around the open space that was tasteful and uncluttered. The simple no-nonsense furnishings were softened by costly artwork and an unusual display that revealed Dakota's environmental interests. Added to the paintings of mountain areas was a lit cabinet holding rocks and minerals and uncut semiprecious gemstones. Honor felt as if she were in a personal gallery.

A few minutes later, Dakota came downstairs, his gray suit jacket flung across the shoulder of his crisp white-on-white shirt. A soft gray-and-mauve tie hung around his neck. She wondered if he always dressed so formally.

He must have guessed at her thoughts because he said, "I have to go into the office this afternoon." He dropped the jacket on the unoccupied couch and secured his collar button. "Staff meeting. Other than that, I'm going to try to get to the bottom of our situation."

"How?" she asked, feeling utterly helpless. "I checked my answering machine three times since this morning. Nothing. Why not?"

He was looking at his reflection in the display cabinet as he looped one end of the tie around the other. "They probably weren't satisfied with what you gave them. They want you to sweat."

"They've succeeded."

Before she could become too morose, he asked, "So, anything interesting happen this morning?" Finished with his tie, he sat on the couch opposite.

"I assume you know Andrew Vaughn."

"Unfortunately."

"Well, he stormed into Willard Zahniser's office just as the meeting was about to get started and demanded Zahniser talk to him right then."

"And?"

"Zahniser stepped into the hall with him." Honor noted that Dakota's eyebrows shot up in surprise.

"Their voices were raised just enough to let me hear bits and pieces of the conversation. Vaughn was talking about something being illegal and his taking all the chances."

"Any idea of what he was referring to?"

"Nothing concrete."

"But you suspect it might have something to do with your daughter."

"The thought crossed my mind."

"What about your ex-husband theory?"

"I—I don't know." To be truthful, she'd forgotten about Gary. "I wouldn't put a trick like this past him, but ..."

"But it's too complicated a deal to be orchestrated by someone who isn't more directly involved with the ransom demand," Dakota finished for her.

"I guess," she said, too tired and anxious to know what to believe.

"Why don't we start from scratch," he suggested. "You come to my office with me, and we'll go over the files. Maybe something will trigger a response. A name, an incident."

"All right. Anything that will help."

Dakota studied Honor carefully as he escorted her from the loft. She seemed so emotionally fragile that part of him felt sorry for her. And he was feeling other things as well. While he'd taken her in his arms to comfort her, *he* had become increasingly disturbed, not only physically, but mentally. He needed to be careful so he wouldn't fall into the same trap that he had with Maureen. Of course, he hadn't been warned then, but this time was different.

Honor hadn't exactly been dealing from the top of the deck when she'd given him the slip after breaking into his office to steal those files. Two strikes against her. He wouldn't allow her a third.

The thought of her duplicity, no matter how noble her reason, was making him back off. More than once, he'd been accused of seeing things in black-and-white—that had been Maureen's refrain after she'd betrayed him and then had expected their relationship to continue. What was right was right, he told himself, and wrong was wrong. Breaking the law rather than working within the system was against everything he believed in. So while he would help Honor find her daughter—legally—he couldn't afford to trust her completely.

When they got to the outer hallway, she hesitated and he felt her resistance.

"Forget something?"

Voice tight, she said, "I almost forgot what happened out there not even a half hour ago."

"My car is right down the street, away from the plaza. You won't even have to see those people, assuming they're still around."

Despite his reservations about getting too close, Dakota wrapped an arm around Honor's back for reassurance. No sooner had they exited the building together than he was aware of a camera clicking away. He turned toward the sound and saw Karen Lopinski, reporter for a regional tabloid. She was grinning at him, and her photographer was shooting away.

"Smile, Raferty, you're on *Candid Camera!*"

Chapter Five

Quick as lightning, Dakota lunged toward the photographer and grabbed the camera. In shock, Honor stood staring at the drama playing out before her.

"Hey, what's the big idea?" the photographer demanded. "Give me that!"

But the slightly built young man was no match for Dakota, who easily kept him at bay while opening the back of the camera. He ripped out the film, exposing it to sunlight and destroying the shots the photographer had just taken. Then he calmly returned the camera to its owner, who moaned and immediately checked it over to make sure the mechanism hadn't been damaged.

"Raferty, I should have you arrested!" the woman said hotly.

"Be my guest, Lopinski," Dakota growled, his manner threatening. "You always do what's best for you anyway, no matter the consequence. I had you on my butt once. Don't press me again!"

"I'm not after you. I'm trying to get a story about her," the woman said, pointing to Honor, who went still and felt the blood drain from her face. "She's got star value."

Realizing this Lopinski was none other than the ace reporter for the *Northwest Eye,* Honor cautiously said, "Why?" She feared the other woman had somehow found out about Nora. She thought about appealing to Karen Lopinski as one mother to another, but she somehow couldn't imagine the reporter in that role.

"You just happen to be someone the public wants to know about," the reporter told Honor. "Everyone will be chomping at the bit to read about the Flawless woman and her new lover."

Breathing a sigh of relief that Nora was safe from the headlines for a while longer, Honor started to deny the accusation. "Dakota and I are not—"

"Save it," Dakota interrupted, pulling her away from Lopinski and the photographer and toward the car. "Let her think what she wants," he whispered, "or she'll start nosing around for the real reason we're together."

"Is that any way to treat a lady?" the reporter yelled after them. "I can see the headline now. 'Prominent lobbyist forces actress to his will.'"

Honor took one last look at the small woman, who reminded her of a bulldog. She knew all about tabloid reporters from bitter experience. Once they got something between their jaws, they didn't let go. She'd been their target innumerable times over the past decade.

Once ensconced in his silver Buick Regal, the doors locked against another intrusion into their privacy, she said, "I know it goes with the territory, but I can't believe, now of all times, I've got a reporter after me for a story."

"Maybe you don't. You've been out of the spotlight for a year. And while I always enjoyed your work, I never thought of you as a star. Sorry," he added as if to assuage any hurt feelings.

"I never thought of myself as a star, either," Honor told him. "But you heard what she said."

Dakota pulled the car out of the parking spot. "Do you really think Lopinski's word is more reliable than the garbage she writes?"

"Probably not." Honor sighed in frustration. "Then what *is* she after?"

"I'm not sure. But she's buddy-buddy with Andrew Vaughn. That sleazeball will do anything to win a political issue, even ruin his opposition, if necessary. And Karen Lopinski is more than happy to publish the mud Vaughn slings at his opponents. Scandal sells rags like hers." Dakota turned the car toward his downtown office. "Hmm. Lopinski, Vaughn and Zahniser. It almost sounds as if there's some kind of conspiracy against me personally."

Honor thought about Vaughn's possible involvement, which seemed to make sense after what she'd heard that morning. Indeed the "illegal" might have to do with fishing activities and "taking chances" with her daughter's kidnapping. Whether or not that pointed to a conspiracy against Dakota himself, she wasn't certain. But someone with a lot at stake had to be orchestrating the whole thing. Zahniser?

"Possessing the right information, the opposition could render your lobbying activities ineffectual," she said. "But why would you think it could be personal?"

"Because of Lopinski."

Dakota had said she'd been on him before, but Honor thought better than to ask him about what.

She'd gotten the distinct feeling that he would have liked to have dumped both reporter and photographer in the Sound, if they'd been close enough. Instead, she wisely held her counsel and said, "If she really is after you rather than me."

"She was waiting outside my building."

"But she could have followed me there. I wasn't exactly in any kind of shape to notice."

Dakota didn't argue with that.

When they arrived at the busy offices of Public Interest Lobbying Cooperative, they proceeded past several people directly to Dakota's private inner sanctum. She hadn't taken a really good look at the place the night before, not that she could have seen much by flashlight. But now, while he unlocked the cabinet that he'd mistakenly left open the day before, she had the opportunity.

The outer office was decorated with heavy old furniture like the desk she'd pulled to his door. Probably from a secondhand shop, if she could judge by the scarring on the solid wood pieces. Going one magnificent step better, his office was decorated with restored antiques.

"Very nice," she said, smoothing a hand over a bookcase that was of solid, carved wood.

"Give my little sister the credit. Asia assures me every piece was handmade either in Washington or Oregon at the end of the nineteenth century. She runs an antique shop in Port Townsend."

Honor knew the Victorian town so popular with tourists was perched on the northeastern corner of the Olympic Peninsula, across Puget Sound.

"I've been meaning to visit Port Townsend since I moved to Seattle, but I haven't made the time."

"It's a charming place," he said, dragging out the hanging file. "Like stepping into yesteryear."

To Honor, Dakota seemed like a man who could appreciate doing just that, as much as he must like spending time in the great outdoors, if the art in his loft was any indication. Her gaze swept the prints of old Seattle hung on these walls. Then she sat next to him at a long table whose surface was inlaid with different color woods.

"Before we start, maybe you should bring me up to date on the problem you're currently addressing," she suggested. Though she represented salmon fishers as a spokesperson, she didn't pay much attention to the politics involved.

"Good idea," Dakota said, his large hand resting on the file between them. "Native American fishermen have the right to at least half of the salmon harvest in the waters off Washington, Oregon and Alaska. Federal courts have upheld this privilege on paper several times in the past few decades, but it's up to the states to carry through—to regulate the white fisheries. Enough salmon must reach Indian grounds not only so they can harvest their share, but so there is a sufficient number left to spawn and renew the run."

Honor had known salmon fishing wasn't what it used to be. The average size of any particular variety had been greatly reduced. And some, like chinook and coho, were severely depressed in number due to overfishing.

"So you've found irregularities—white companies taking too much of the catch," she said.

"Exactly. Several years ago, a questionable sting operation was coordinated by the National Marine Fisheries Service and involved state officers from Washington and Oregon. 'SamScam' entrapped a number of Native Americans into selling fish taken out of season. One of them got five years for selling twenty-eight fish."

"My God, isn't that a little harsh?" Honor asked.

"Especially since the men who were tried pointed out that all fifty-three tons taken illegally over fourteen months was approximately the over-quota catch taken by white-owned ocean trollers in a single day."

"And they never get caught?"

"Few and far between. No proof."

"But you've got proof." Honor indicated the files. "Why not give it to the authorities outright and let them take care of the problem? Let them bring suit against the companies."

"That'll happen soon, I hope. We're going for more than arrests—we want stricter laws making associated industries equally liable. Once the blame and the consequences can be spread more evenly, we may have a chance of putting a hold on illegal fishing—the theory being, if they can't sell it, they won't catch it. I'm going to let you look at statements made by people who have witnessed illegal fishing, but you have to promise me you won't reveal their names to anyone."

"I promise."

Dakota's expression was intense when he said, "On your daughter's life, Honor, because if this information gets into the wrong hands, it could mean other lives. Whoever is trying to stop this campaign is serious."

Blood drained from her face, Honor nodded. "I don't want anyone hurt."

They spent the next hour carefully going through the files. Company names, dates, witnesses—they were all there. Unfortunately, she was no closer to an answer than before. "Nothing rings a bell," she said with disappointment. "Nothing."

"Well, your taking a look isn't time wasted. Just keep your eyes and your ears open." Dakota gathered the materials and placed them in the hanging folder, which he then carried back to the file cabinet. "Maybe something will come up over at NCSC that can help us."

Honor knew that even if Nora were released, she couldn't pick up and walk away from this—not that she was passing moral judgment on the men who were making a living by overfishing. Unemployment was a real problem and she wasn't sure she could place healthy future fish harvests over present-day basic human needs. People had to take care of their families.

The kidnappers were another story, however. They were the real criminals, and Honor wanted to see them caught not only for her sake, but for Dakota's. And if she inadvertently helped his cause, so be it.

"Am I interrupting?"

Startled, Honor turned around and came face-to-face with the dark-haired woman who'd been in the office the night before. She shifted guiltily, even though the young woman couldn't possibly identify her as the one who broke in. Not that anyone even knew about her illegal entry, since she and Dakota had covered her tracks before leaving.

Dakota made introductions. "Janet Ingel, Honor Bright. Janet is one of my fellow lobbyists."

"And Honor works for your competition," Janet said, her blue eyes never wavering. She met Honor's gaze squarely. "How curious that the two of you are huddled in here together. Or have you quit your job as spokesperson for NCSC?"

"No, I haven't."

Now how was she going to explain her presence? Honor wondered. She thought quickly, but Janet seemed to dismiss her as she addressed Dakota.

"Can I talk to you for a minute?"

"About?"

"Maybe I should leave," Honor said when Janet glanced back at her.

"No, stay put." Dakota gave his fellow lobbyist a questioning expression and repeated, "About . . . ?"

Obviously realizing she wasn't about to get him alone, Janet frowned, and her pretty features became as severe as the rest of her. Her dark suit was tailored without a hint of softness. Likewise, her long black hair was pulled back and tightly secured.

"About a new client I want to take on." Her tone was defensive, as if she expected him to object. "A group of shelters for women and their children called Safe-houses wants to hire PILC to lobby for financial support. This is very important to me, Dakota."

"I'm always open to taking on new clients," he said reasonably.

"Then you'll give me your support at the meeting this afternoon?"

"If your report convinces me this is a worthwhile group."

"Then you *won't* promise your support?" Janet asked, her anger barely controlled.

"I'll listen with an open mind."

"As open as someone with your background can be," she muttered, stalking out of the office.

Dakota sighed, the sound a mix of frustration and thankfulness, and threw up his hands.

"You two don't get along?" Honor asked.

"Not very often. Janet holds my background against me, as you may have guessed. She pulled herself up out of poverty, put herself through school and is now working in the public interest, trying to help others do the same."

"A bright woman."

"And at twenty-four, a bright future ahead of her. If only she could get rid of that blind spot when it comes to people who had it easier than she did."

Honor knew Dakota's father was a judge and that the Raferty siblings had lacked for nothing while they were growing up. Sydney had told her that Dakota could have gone to any law school he chose and that the family money had paid for his first campaign for state congressman. But neither of those things made him less worthwhile a person.

"You could be doing anything you wanted with your background and contacts," she said. "But you choose to work here, to help organizations who don't have a lot of money, rather than going for the big bucks and power by working with big business. Janet Ingel should give you a break."

Dakota cracked a smile at that. "I doubt she'll ever be convinced. I think I made a mistake when I gave Asia a free hand in here. This office is a constant reminder of where I came from."

"It's not anything to be ashamed of."

"No, it isn't. I'm very proud of my family. My parents instilled great values in all three of their children."

"Maybe Janet will realize that someday."

"Maybe," he echoed, though he didn't sound convinced.

The bond of camaraderie made Honor feel lighthearted for a moment—until she remembered her reason for being with Dakota. Her inner smile slipped away.

"Can I use your telephone?" she asked.

"Go ahead."

With shaky fingers, Honor punched out her own number and with baited breath waited to hear about her daughter. But once again, no message.

"They didn't call," she said softly as she dropped the receiver into the cradle. "Why don't they call?"

Dakota rounded his desk and placed his hands lightly on her shoulders. "You look exhausted."

"I could use some sleep," she admitted. She'd never felt so tired in her life.

"Do you have any reason to go back to the NCSC offices?"

"Not until tomorrow."

"Then I suggest you go home and hit the sack until they do call." Dakota turned her toward the door and escorted her through the outer office. "I'll come by later," he said softly. "If you hear anything, you let me know immediately."

She nodded. She couldn't go this alone. She'd thought she was strong, but the longer this went on, the more defenseless she felt.

Dakota left her at the elevator. And then she was on her own. Too tired to walk even a few blocks, she took a taxi to her car. She would have taken it all the way home, but she might need to pick up Nora.

If they ever called. . . .

KING CRAWLEY INSPECTED the contents of the envelope carefully. He was definitely not impressed. There wasn't a thing here he could use.

"What the hell is this you think you're giving me?"

"It's what she gave us."

"It's not enough. It's less than that. You understand what I'm tellin' you? This is nothing." He threw the envelope back at his visitor and was gratified to see the tremble in the fingers that retrieved it. "I thought you were serious. You wanna be my friend or not?"

"Yes, Mr. Crawley, o-of course I do. I am your friend."

Crawley's glare was purposely steady and filled with threat. Then he leaned forward, made his voice deceptively pleasant by contrast. "Friends do what they have to for each other, right? Especially if they want something important in return?"

Eyes wide, face flushed, his visitor managed to choke out, "Y-yes."

Crawley smiled. He still had it—the power to inspire fear. He could smell it on a person. This one pretended to be tough, but underneath, the fear grew like maggots. Even if his visitor was having second thoughts, it was too late to back out, and they both knew it. He had control. His smile broadened and the smell blossomed, tantalizing his nostrils. He almost laughed at the pitiful display of cowardice. His circumstances didn't matter. He would have his power until the end.

"So what do you want me to do?" came the whispered question—just as he'd known it would.

"Get me something I can use."

The fingers tightened on the envelope. "You mean, do it myself?"

Crawley leaned back and gave an exaggerated sigh. "Only if you're damned stupid. The first rule is to let other people get their hands dirty whenever possible. Our Little Miss Movie Star is going to do exactly what you want . . . if you play your cards right."

"She did try to do what we asked."

"Tell her to try harder," Crawley insisted. "Use the kid any way you have to."

He could tell that suggestion didn't sit well. The face before him paled and the fingers squeezed the life out of that envelope.

But in the end, Crawley knew, his "friend" would do whatever it took.

A SHRILL SOUND MADE HONOR jerk up in bed and lunge for the phone. But when she picked up the receiver, all she heard was the dial tone.

The noise came again—the doorbell.

Sliding out of bed, Honor rubbed the grogginess from her eyes and glanced at the alarm clock. A quarter to six. She'd slept for nearly five hours. The doorbell shrilled a third time as she stumbled down the stairs. She glanced toward the answering machine in case the call had come in without her hearing.

The red electronic eye stared back at her steadily.

No calls . . . no Nora.

But Dakota stood on the porch, body tensed, face pressed to the curtained glass in the door. When he spotted her, he relaxed and stepped back.

Seeing her own reflection, Honor ran a hand through the tangle of curls that was going every which way. The moment she'd come home, she'd jumped in the shower. She'd pulled on terry shorts and a tank top but hadn't bothered to dry her hair before throwing herself across the bed.

She opened the door. Dakota took one look at her face and said, "No news."

"I would have called."

"I wasn't so sure."

"You can trust me, Dakota, honestly." Honor closed the door behind him and admitted, "I need you."

He stared at her for a moment—the way a man looks at a woman—making her uncomfortable. She brushed by him, intending to sit in the rocking chair.

"Have you eaten?" he finally asked.

She turned to him and realized he was staring at her long, bare legs. "Yesterday...I—I think." He was making her nervous. She didn't know what to do with her hands, so she crossed her arms in front of her chest.

"What's in the refrigerator?"

"Hot dogs. Nora's favorite. And some fresh fish. At least, it was fresh when I bought it Saturday."

Dakota winced. "How about if I call out and order Chinese?"

"Sure. Whatever you want. I'm not really hungry."

"But you're going to eat anyway." Before she could protest, he added, "You'll do it for Nora. You're going to need your strength. That means your body needs fuel to keep it going. Where's your phone book?"

"By the telephone. And if you look in the drawer, you'll find a couple of menus, including Chinese. You order, I'll get dressed."

"What you're wearing is fine with me."

But it wasn't with Honor. She felt awkward, too exposed to his male interest, which Dakota didn't bother to hide. She would feel better if more of her were covered.

"I'll be down in a few minutes," she told him, trying to ignore his gaze following her up the stairs.

Once dressed in white jeans and a green shirt, she sat at her dressing table and began the difficult task of combing through her naturally curly hair. While she worked, she thought about Dakota, about the fact that she was fighting what should be a very normal attraction.

Nothing was normal about this situation, about the way she met him.

Nothing.

She winced as her pick stuck in her hair and she had to work a tangle free by hand. Finally, she was able to pull a wide-toothed comb through the copper curls. She gathered the masses of hair, fastening the fall in back with a green banana clip. Not bothering with makeup or shoes, she left the bedroom for the stairs, where she stopped halfway down and stared at Dakota.

He sat relaxed on the couch, the top of his shirt unbuttoned, tie loose, sleeves rolled up. His head lolled back against the cushion and his eyes were closed. A gorgeous, gorgeous man, she admitted.

But not one for her.

Past experience with that sleazeball Andrew Vaughn had Honor convinced that lobbyists would do whatever was necessary to help their side win—in Vaughn's case, maybe even kidnapping. While Dakota seemed to be an honorable man by comparison, she hadn't seen him in action. For all she knew, he was equally ruthless in his own way.

Didn't his forcing her to agree to work with him to trap the villains prove that?

Dakota should have offered to give her the salmon-fishing files to free her daughter from the first, she thought resentfully. What was winning his side of some issue—no matter how noble—if it meant putting a child's life on the line?

A little voice reminded her of the promise she'd made not to reveal any names seen in the file. Dakota had been trying to protect those people, had intimated *their* lives might be at stake. But that didn't soften the resentment she felt at not having her daughter safe and sound in her arms.

The kidnappers knew she was holding out. Of that she was certain. They were trying to drive her crazy with not knowing what was happening to Nora, so that when they did call, she would do anything they asked. Anything except reveal the names of those witnesses, she amended. She was willing to be ruthless where her daughter was concerned, but she couldn't knowingly endanger anyone else.

That determined, she descended the rest of the way into the living room.

Dakota's eyes flew open and he straightened. "Food should be here in a few minutes."

"Good." Though she still wasn't hungry. "I'll set the table."

"I'll help." He started to rise.

"No!"

The force of the word sent him tumbling back to his seat. He stared at her in surprise. Well, let him stare. He wasn't going to get to her. She had other, more important things to think about.

And it would have been impossible to keep her mind off her daughter even if she'd tried, Honor realized. The house was filled with reminders. Nora's favorite book of fairy tales on the dining room table; the mobile Nora had picked out hanging in the breakfast nook; the Teenage Mutant Ninja Turtles glass in the kitchen cabinet.

Everywhere she turned, Honor saw images of her daughter. She didn't know how she managed to set the table without breaking down completely. She was placing flatware on the table when she realized Dakota was staring at her. Had he been doing so all along?

As if to prove to herself that he should be off limits, she asked, "So what made you decide to become a public-interest lobbyist?" hoping he would reveal something about himself that would allow her to disrespect him.

But when he said, "Idealism, I guess," she didn't know what to think.

And his smile made it obvious that he thought she was looking for a safe topic.

"I'm looking for my niche, the place where I can do the most good," he went on. "I didn't have to fight to make my way in this world, so I can concentrate my efforts on trying to make it a better place. With hard work and luck, maybe I'll make a difference."

Though it was difficult to resent a man who purported to have such purpose, Honor couldn't help herself. "So you haven't succeeded yet?"

Dakota gave her a wary look as if he finally sensed she was doing more than making small talk. "In minor ways. Reynard Stirling has been after me to run for the U.S. Senate. I've been giving it serious thought."

"Because you can do more good at a national level than working directly with the people in your state?"

"Something like that."

His clipped tone told her the discussion was at an end. Feeling a little guilty, Honor didn't push it. For all she knew, Dakota was exactly what he made himself out to be. The doorbell and the arrival of dinner saved her from any awkwardness. Dakota took care of the delivery person while Honor retrieved a bottle of cola from the refrigerator.

As they ate, she found herself relaxing with Dakota despite her doubts. He was interested in hearing about life in the fast lane. Now she was on the spot, talking about her work.

"In addition to being a grind, show business is emotionally exhausting." Though she hadn't thought she had an appetite, she spooned a second helping of Princess Prawns onto her plate and took a couple more pot stickers for good measure. Dakota was doing a thorough job of finishing anything she couldn't eat. "You're always on, always worried that next week you won't be able to get work."

"So what was the lure?"

She took a bite of food and shrugged. "I was born in L.A. I guess dreams of stardom are part of the territory. My break came right after high school graduation—a small role in a big movie. It was a fluke, really, but I was hooked by the glamour that went along with the hard work. And I was noticed by the powers that be. While I never became a big star as you so astutely pointed out, I always had work. Decent roles in movies, guest shots on television."

"Being the spokesperson for Flawless. Why the change?"

"Nora and a failed marriage. It was a chance to stay in one spot for a while. But before I knew it, I was divorced and on location for another movie, dragging my daughter along. And then there was another offer. And another. One day, I took a good look at my hectic life and realized that if I didn't slow down, I would miss something irreplaceable...and maybe make a mess of Nora's life while I was at it."

"So you took the job with the NCSC." Dakota gave her an intent look when he asked, "Don't you miss the excitement?"

"Sometimes," she admitted. "But I figured I could give it up for a couple of years, at least until Nora was in school. She needed some stability in her life. If I still want to go back in the next couple of years, I'll try for steady employment in one area, maybe a small part in a series. That is, assuming I still have what it takes to get work. I'm not getting any younger, and people in Hollywood have short memories."

"As far as I'm concerned, you haven't lost anything important," Dakota assured her. "Except a husband."

"Well, that's what happens when you get fooled by the movies. Gary was my leading man." Honor speared the pan-fried dumpling over and over as though she could let out her hostility toward her ex-husband on it.

"I thought he was the only good thing that came out of the one disaster I starred in. Shows what kind of a judge of character I am. It wasn't until I was seven-months pregnant that I learned Gary was no real-life hero. I discovered he had playmates both on location and near home—he'd had them practically since the honeymoon."

"The man was a fool."

Ignoring the compliment, Honor said, "And I was stupid enough to believe that he would change. Gary agreed to be faithful, I agreed to stay—until I learned that he hadn't stuck to his end of the bargain." She was tired of talking about herself, about memories that were painful. "What about you? Have you ever been married?"

"Almost."

"Almost only counts in horseshoes," Honor said. "What happened?"

"Do you know my father is a judge?"

She nodded. "Sydney told me."

"Well, he was presiding over an important case, the trial of a Seattle racketeer named King Crawley. Maureen had been working as a public defender. She used her connection with me to get a job working with Crawley's lawyers. No doubt they hired her hoping to get an edge on the case. She never told me. I found out watching the five o'clock news. I was stunned by the story and the speculation that went with it."

"How awful. She pretended to be in love with you only so she could use you."

"More like she used me in spite of our relationship," Dakota countered. "I believe Maureen really did love me in her own selfish way. Afterward, she couldn't believe that I would hold what she saw as a savvy professional move against her. She swore she never meant to feed the firm any privileged information—although she realized that was why she was hired. I knew I never could trust her again, though, so I broke it off."

The telephone ringing saved Honor from having to find a consoling follow-up.

The fork dropped from her suddenly lifeless fingers, and she had trouble finding her legs. "It's them," she choked out, awkwardly pushing herself up to her feet.

Her pulse doubled in the seconds it took her to get to the phone that rang a second time. Dakota was right beside her as she lifted the receiver.

Honor's heart banged against her ribs. *Let it be them. Please, let it be them.*

"Hello," she said cautiously, never in the world expecting to hear her daughter's voice.

"Mommy!" Nora cried. "I miss you."

Honor would have lost control if Dakota hadn't been there to support her. He quickly wrapped an arm around her shoulders, pressed an ear close to hers so he could hear.

Softly, in a voice that she didn't recognize as her own she said, "I miss you, too, peaches." Now what? Her mind swirled with possibilities. "Nora, honey, are you all right?"

Chapter Six

"'Course I am," Nora replied to Honor's relief. "But you promised no more movies for a long, long time."

"What?"

"You promised," Nora repeated petulantly.

Honor realized the kidnappers must have told her daughter she was on a movie shoot. "Yes, sweetheart, I did promise," she said, giving Dakota a sideways glance. "But sometimes grown-ups have to do things we don't want to do."

The petulance faded from Nora's voice only to be replaced by longing when she asked, "Am I gonna see you soon?"

"I hope so," Honor said fervently. Her eyes began to sting. "Just as quick as possible. I love you, peaches." She heard a muffled noise and an electronic click at the other end. "Nora? Nora?"

"Settle down, Ms. Bright," came a hollow, genderless voice. It belonged to the kidnapper with whom she'd spoken before. "Your daughter is fine...for now."

"What do you mean, 'for now'? You got your damn papers!" Honor bluffed. She felt Dakota tense beside her. "Tell me where I can find my child."

"I'll tell you when you give us some *real* information. The stuff you dropped off won't do."

"What do you mean?" The only reason she didn't panic was the reassuring squeeze Dakota gave her arm. "I got you a report, pictures—"

"Useless!" the electronic voice shouted. "But then, maybe you don't know that. Maybe you're not playing a game with us. If I thought you were..."

"No, I'm not playing a game." She was deadly serious. The implied threat made her heart pound faster. "I just want my daughter back."

"And you'll get her when we get what we want."

She moved away from Dakota far enough to give him a stricken look. "I—I don't know..."

"Do it! You have two hours to obtain the information and bring it to the drop-off site."

"Where? The dock?"

"The outdoor soup kitchen a few blocks east of Pike Place Market. Do you know the area?"

"Yes." More than once driving in her car she'd passed the place where many of the homeless were fed each night. "Where am I supposed to leave the information?"

"Just stick around the distribution area," the voice ordered. "We'll find you. And Ms. Bright...this time, don't play 'I Spy.' It wouldn't be good for your health...or your daughter's."

"Wait a minute! What if I can't—"

A click interrupted her panicked response. The line went dead. Slowly, she let down the receiver. Two hours. She checked the clock on the mantel, then met Dakota's aquamarine gaze.

"You heard?"

He nodded. "Enough, anyway."

"What am I going to do?"

He swiped a lock of ash-blond hair from his forehead. "You're going to take some of the real information, things that won't identify any of our informants."

A little of the weight lifted from her heart. "You'll really give me enough to satisfy them?"

"I hope so, but there's one condition," Dakota told her. "This time you don't try to lose me."

"I won't. Nora wasn't returned to me last time, so what good would it do me to try to fool you again?"

"No good, whatsoever."

Honor only hoped that cooperating wasn't the biggest mistake she'd ever made.

DAKOTA WAS GLAD he'd brought the documents home. Less of a hassle, and he could change clothes while he was there. He donned worn jeans and a navy T-shirt, the kind of outfit that would guarantee him a measure of anonymity. Then he rejoined Honor, who paced the length of his living room.

"Calm down," he urged. "You have to be level-headed and in control to carry this thing off."

"I know. I'll be fine. I can do anything once I set my mind to it," she muttered as if to convince herself rather than him. "I *have* to do it."

Dakota removed a painting from the wall to reveal a hidden safe. Honor continued to pace. He felt her eyes on him as he turned the dial, but when he glanced her way, she quickly looked toward the windows as if embarrassed that he'd caught her. He popped open the door and removed the folder containing the incriminating information. He sorted through everything, selecting a few revealing photos in addition to a damaging report that, thankfully, didn't name names.

"This should do it," he said, returning the rest of the information to the safe and spinning the dial. He wasn't about to be careless at this stage of the game.

She stopped in the middle of the floor and said, "God, I want this to be over."

As did he.

He wasn't crazy about working with a woman he couldn't completely trust.

Honor was quiet and still as they drove through the dark across the downtown area, but Dakota could sense her mounting tension. He parked on a side street near the market, several blocks from the drop-off site. In silence, they set off for the soup kitchen, which was located on a block whose buildings were being demolished.

Envelope gripped tightly to her side, Honor was practically running.

"Slow down," he told her. "Let me get ahead of you so they don't see us together."

She gripped his arm and stopped dead. "What are you planning on doing?"

"I'm planning on following the pick-up."

He tried not to wince as her nails bit into his flesh. Her face pulled into a horrified expression. She was terrified, and he couldn't blame her.

"My God, Dakota, what if they see you?"

"They won't be expecting me."

"What about Nora?"

"Honor, no guarantees, remember?" He calmly removed her hand from his arm and cradled it between both of his. "Even if they get everything they want, you might never see your daughter again. But the kidnappers aren't your garden-variety criminals who will take off once they get the ransom. They have something at stake right here in Seattle, so I don't think they want the police on their backs."

"But what if you're wrong?"

Dakota didn't know how to respond to that. He would feel responsible if anything happened to that little girl—whether he acted or not. He felt compelled to do so, to turn the tables on the cowards who would use a child so callously. Even if they let Nora go as promised, he didn't want to let *them* go.

But was that his decision to make?

Again he reminded himself that Nora wasn't his daughter.

"Do you want me to stop right now?" he asked Honor. "I can. Just say the word and I'll let you make the delivery on your own."

"No, please. I can't . . . I told you I need you."

Honor chewed her bottom lip. The streetlight glinted off the unshed tears in her eyes, and he could read the pleading in them. Dakota restrained himself from taking her in his arms to try to comfort her. Her falling apart now wouldn't help anything.

"You could still go to the police," he told her. "That's what I would suggest."

"No police," she whispered. "We'll do it your way. You go ahead. I'll wait a minute, then follow."

"Are you sure?" he asked.

She nodded once. "Positive. Be careful."

Dakota felt Honor's eyes on his back as he walked away from her and crossed to the opposite side of the street. He only hoped he wasn't being a damn fool.

If anything did happen to Nora because of him, he would never forgive himself.

Honor lost sight of Dakota before getting to the drop-off site. If he was among the homeless who waited in line for their daily meal or lounged on the curb eating and talking, she couldn't spot him. With a sense of unease, she stepped near the distribution table, where a half dozen volunteers cheerfully served food and joked with the regulars.

Misfortune wasn't gender or age conscious, she noted. There were men and women younger than she, while others were old enough to be her grandparents. And the children . . . dear Lord, so many homeless children. Eyes stinging, she turned away from them.

Being so close to so many people who had nothing made her uncomfortable. Though she was no millionaire, she had so much by comparison that her good fortune embarrassed her.

Besides which, her presence was alien in this environment. Dozens of eyes turned to stare. Wearing the green shirt, white jeans and a matching jacket, she still stuck out like a sore thumb among these people, many of whom wore everything they owned on their backs.

A man broke from the line, grabbing her immediate attention. He was dressed in greasy workpants, a torn T-shirt and a lightweight jacket that had seen better days. A baseball cap crowning his head was the newest, cleanest item he wore, incongruous with the rest of him. As he approached her, she stiffened.

Her first thought was that he was going to hit on her for money. Her second, that if she weren't alone, the kidnappers wouldn't make the rendezvous.

What to do?

When the man stopped barely a foot away and discarded something on the ground, however, he asked, "That it?" in a low voice.

She stared, but it was too dark to make out much and the cap and grime helped hide the man's face.

"Is...that...it?" Keeping his voice low—to disguise it?—he enunciated each word carefully, as if she were slow-witted.

"Is it what?"

The words came out sharper than Honor had intended. She wanted to make sure she didn't give the information to the wrong man. He was taller and broader than she remembered—though she had only gotten a quick glimpse of the person at the pier. Perhaps he had been the one watching, the one who'd knocked her unconscious.

"The files, Ms. Bright, what do you think?"

Her fingers flexed on the envelope. "My daughter...?"

"All in good time," he said, holding out his hand.

Having no choice, unable to think of a reason to delay the inevitable, she handed over the envelope. Before she could blink, the man blended back into the mass of homeless, nearly knocking over a woman in an ankle-length winter coat in his hurry to disappear into the crowd.

Frantically, Honor looked for Dakota, but she didn't spot him immediately. When she finally identified him by his blond head, which stuck above the ones surrounding him, he was twenty yards or so away. He was searching the crowd himself. He must have seen the transaction.

Her instincts were to run to him, to help him find the man.

Her heart pounded as she stood frozen, helpless, knowing she had to stay where she was or risk her daughter's life.

DAKOTA SIDLED UP TO A MAN wearing a billed cap. It wasn't until the guy turned toward him with a toothless grin that Dakota could see by the old and grizzled face that this was the wrong person.

He methodically continued searching the crowd until he spotted another, younger man breaking from the food line and heading toward an abandoned building already falling to the wrecker's ball. Dakota went after him, hands in his pockets, shoulders slumped in imitation of the homeless who mainly kept to themselves, shy and distrusting.

He narrowed the gap and was soon close enough to see the man push aside a large piece of lumber blocking a street-level door, then slide through the opening and disappear. Dakota picked up his pace, took longer strides without actually running.

The last thing he needed to do was to draw attention to himself.

A minute later, he was inside the old warehouse, peering into the darkness. He waited until his eyes adjusted before stepping forward cautiously. One side of the building had already been demolished. Light from the street and the moonlit sky shone in, casting a pale glow over the rubble-strewn floor.

A noise alerted him to another presence. Above him, north side of the building.

A wide staircase took Dakota to the second-floor landing, where he paused and listened again. All was quiet until the wail of a siren from the outside streets signaled the approach of a police car. He used the cover to move toward the central area of the building, which was split in two by the open elevator shaft.

Standing in the shadow of a broad building support, he waited. As the siren faded away, he heard a minute noise. Directionless. The shuffle of paper?

For a moment, Dakota felt like a cat to the kidnapper's mouse.

Then reality set in.

He had no weapon, no way of defending himself, while the kidnapper was surely armed. The thought made him sweat. He wasn't afraid of much—but a little fear was healthy. It would keep him alert.

And hopefully alive.

Stealthily, he circumvented the partially caged elevator shaft and approached a wide doorway that led to another section of the building. He was careful to make no sound of his own. But from the dark interior of the room ahead came a muffled cry—that of a child—followed by a soft, feminine, "S-s-h-h."

Dakota stopped dead in his tracks.

"Ma-a!" another child insisted, the word cut off abruptly.

Though he knew this was not his prey, Dakota was unable to stop himself from drawing closer to the room. He hesitated in the doorway, barely able to make out a woman huddled with her two children under a covering of newspapers. She had a hand clamped over either small mouth.

"Please, mister, don't hurt us," the woman begged. Her voice shook with real fear. "We don't mean no harm. Just needed a place to sleep. We ain't got nothing fer you to steal."

The smaller child started whimpering and Dakota had difficulty speaking.

"I'm going now," he told her. "You're safe." For tonight, he added silently. "I don't mean you or your children any harm."

Distressed by their plight, he backed away. Then he spun around, suddenly in a hurry to leave this pitiful place of refuge, wondering how long they'd been there, wondering what that woman would do to shelter her children when the building came down within the week.

Dakota shook his head at another seemingly insolvable problem, which for a moment had eclipsed his losing the man he'd been following. No doubt the guy had been covering his tracks and had gone out another door or window.

What in the world was he going to tell Honor? She'd been counting on him.

He was preoccupied with finding a gentle way to let her down as he crossed in front of the elevator shaft and headed for the stairs. Passing a building support, he saw a flash of movement from the corner of his eye. Before he could turn, he was jumped from behind by a man of his own size. They fell to the floor together, and Dakota got a glimpse of a billed cap.

So the bastard hadn't gotten away, after all!

Dakota grunted when the man placed a well-sized fist to his side. He thrust back an elbow. Contact. The grip on him loosened and Dakota scrambled, his feet slipping on and tripping over the loose rubble strewn across the floor. The other man was up nearly as quickly.

They danced around each other, throwing punches that mostly met thin air.

Dakota backed off and tried to regroup, to formulate a plan of action. Before he could do so, the kidnapper rushed him headfirst.

He tried to stop the onslaught, but the man had momentum on his side. Head connected with solar plexus and they both went flying in the direction of the elevator shaft. Dakota hooked his hands under the man's armpits and sent him off balance, then went down on top of him, face-to-face.

Not that he could actually identify the criminal.

In an attempt to do so, he grabbed at the cap, but his wrist was caught in a tight grip, stopping him. The man punched him in the jaw and Dakota saw stars for a few seconds, long enough to lose the advantage. Even as the other man rolled out from under him, however, Dakota quickly frisked him for a gun.

No weapon, at least none he could find.

And, curiously enough, no envelope of information!

The kidnapper was the first to his feet this time, bringing with him a length of rotting timber. As Dakota rose, the other man swung and caught him across the throat.

Air temporarily cut off, Dakota went spinning toward the yawning chasm of the elevator shaft.

Only by sheer tenaciousness was he able to grab on to the caged side, which rattled and groaned under his weight. Gasping for breath, he was barely able to hold himself from falling as wind whistled up the empty shaft. His heart pumped madly at the whispered threat. His body dangled over the opening, one foot barely keeping contact with solid flooring.

An incident from his youth flashed through Dakota's mind. He and a friend had explored an abandoned building despite Sydney's warning. His sister had "seen" the accident days before it had happened. The rotting floor had given way beneath his feet. Jagged wood had caught on his clothing, saving him from certain death, but only after ripping open his side. Twenty-seven stitches.

This time, he probably wouldn't be so lucky.

When the death blow didn't come, Dakota realized he was alone. The other man had slithered into the night like the low creature he was.

With the oxygen flowing more naturally through his aching throat, Dakota set about readjusting his weight to another bout of metallic creaking and groaning from the ancient cage. He pushed himself onto both feet and took a deep if painful breath of relief that was short-lived.

He still had to face Honor and tell her that instead of following the man to his associates—and to Nora—he'd merely warned the criminals that she had help. Failure didn't come easily to a man who was used to success.

HONOR WANDERED THE LENGTH of the soup-kitchen line, wondering if Dakota had succeeded in following the courier to wherever the kidnappers were holding Nora. Not likely. The man probably had a vehicle waiting for him, and taxis were never to be found when you really needed one.

So what was taking him so long? she wondered. Should she wait for him to return?

The thought that something might have happened to him in that abandoned building chilled her. She didn't need Dakota Raferty on her conscience. Perhaps she should go after him. Then, again, her impulsiveness might screw things up if he had everything under control.

What to do?

She found herself near the distribution area, in the same spot where she had waited for her contact. Remembering the man throwing something away, she looked down and spotted a cigar stub that had been trampled.

"We just opened a new shelter," a smiling volunteer told her. "Here's some information."

The young man pushed a flyer at Honor. Taking the handout, she automatically stuffed it into her jacket pocket.

"Thanks."

The strain of waiting was exhausting her, and a stretch of vacant curb looked inviting. She settled herself in and told herself to be patient.

She wasn't alone for long. A young woman with dirty blond hair sat down a yard away, one hand balancing a plate of food while the other secured a child to her breast. The little girl's arms were thrown around her mother's neck, her feet twined around her waist.

"Honey, wake up," the mother said, setting the plate down on the curb. "It's time to eat."

She resettled the child on her lap and gave the sleepy flaxen-haired girl the first bite of the stew.

Emotions filling her at the reminder of her own daughter, Honor watched, then was embarrassed when the young woman's gaze shyly met hers.

"Hi. I'm Andrea and this is Kathy."

"Honor."

The woman took a mouthful of food and spooned another for her child. "You're new here, aren't you?"

"Sort of." Honor forced the words past the lump in her throat. "Have you been..." She couldn't for the life of her say *homeless*. It was inconceivable that a woman as young as this one—and with a small child—should have no safe place to go. "Have you been coming here long?"

"A couple of weeks."

"What happened?"

"My husband ran out on me and Kathy. He hadn't paid the rent in a couple of months. I couldn't find work. I tried to get welfare, but that takes a while...and a place to live. I was on the street before it came through. Now I'm not sure what's going to happen to us."

"You don't have any family?"

"None that wants us," the woman said, taking some more stew. "But we're on the list for that new shelter. We'll be all right if we can get in, won't we, Kathy?"

Trying to think of a way she could help Andrea and her daughter, Honor caught sight of Dakota coming toward her. He was alone and looked worse for wear.

Heart thundering, she rose and fumbled in her jeans pocket for her wallet. Emptying its contents, she shoved nearly a hundred dollars at Andrea. "Take this."

"No, I couldn't."

"Do it for her," Honor insisted. "Give your little girl someplace safe to sleep for a night or two." She was only doing what she hoped someone else might do for Nora.

Andrea nodded and her eyes filled as she took the bills. "How can I ever thank you? Where do you live? I swear I'll repay you."

"Just take care of her," Honor whispered, rushing to Dakota, who waited a few yards away.

She immediately realized he'd been in a fight. His hair was a mess, his clothes filthy. Faint bruises were blossoming on his jaw and neck. Fear squeezed her chest, making it difficult to speak.

"My God, what happened?"

Dakota pulled her away from the distribution area, which by now, had cleared. The volunteers were packing up, getting ready to leave.

"I lost him, but not before he figured out you have someone helping you. I screwed up. I'm sorry."

His expression was pained and not, she suspected, from the physical abuse he'd taken at the hands of some madman. He feared he'd made the situation worse. But what could be worse other than the unthinkable?

Honor felt the blood drain from her face and her lips were stiff—frozen—as she faintly asked, "Now what? Do you think they'll still let Nora go if they're satisfied with the documents?"

"I hope so. Assuming the bastard didn't lose them.'

"What?"

"We got pretty close," Dakota told her. "No way did he have that envelope on him. I suppose he could have hid it somewhere in the warehouse when he realized was following him. Let's hope nothing happens to the contents before he comes back for it.''

Honor thought quickly. "Or he could have passed the information to an accomplice." She was already searching the area that had thinned considerably. "After he took the envelope, he headed back through the food line and bumped into a woman wearing a long winter coat. He could have passed it to her and then acted as a decoy in case I called in the police. I don't see the woman anywhere."

"How good a look did you get at her?"

"Not good," she admitted. "Not at him, either. I tried, but it was impossible."

"Is there *anything* you can remember?" he probed. "Something you saw? Heard? A regional accent, maybe?"

"No, but he didn't sound natural. He spoke in this very low tone, as though he were trying to disguise his voice." Her gaze strayed to the spot where she'd met with the villain. "And he threw away a cigar stub." A thought crystallizing and making her eyes widen, she looked back at Dakota. "Gary smokes cigars."

"Surely you would recognize your own ex-husband."

"You would think so, but even I could be fooled. His size was right. And as I told you before, Gary is a great actor." Honor took real hope for the first time that night. "With a good disguise, he could lose himself in a part."

"Or it might not have been your ex, at all," Dakota countered. "Andrew Vaughn also smokes cigars."

"No." She shook her head. "I don't think it was Vaughn. He couldn't be that good an actor."

"How do you know that?" Dakota challenged her, his expression pitying.

Anger, strong and heated, filled Honor. "Why don't you want to believe my ex-husband could have stolen Nora?" she demanded.

If Gary was the kidnapper, at least he wouldn't hurt his own daughter. She could take hope in that fact. Turning her back on Dakota, she strode in the direction of Pike Place Market.

"Where are you going?" he asked, his long legs easily keeping stride with hers.

"Home. I'm going to call my ex-husband in L.A. He said he was back from location and he didn't mention a new project, but I'll lay odds that he won't be there."

Chapter Seven

"Hiya, babe. Love ya," the familiar voice on the answering machine intoned. "Do it!" A sharp beep followed.

"Gary, this is Honor," she said angrily before realizing hanging up and letting her ex-husband think it was a wrong number or a salesperson might have been a wise move. What kind of message was she supposed to leave now? Honor wondered. "Uh...talk to you soon," she gasped out before slamming the receiver in its cradle.

"I take it he wasn't there."

"I told you he wouldn't be," she said, triumph all mixed up with nerves.

"He could be out."

"Right, delivering those papers to his cohorts."

Honor had decided why Gary had wanted the salmon fishing files—neither for himself, since that wouldn't make any sense, nor just to throw her off the track, but as payment to interested parties for helping him get even with her. Now if only she could figure out who his connection was and how he'd linked up with the other guilty party or parties.

"You're upset," Dakota stated.

"Of course I'm upset!"

"And not thinking straight."

Sensing he didn't follow her logic, she insisted, "It has to be Gary!" as if by her very intensity she could convince him.

Dakota took her in his arms. He pressed his face against her hair, made soothing sounds meant to comfort. His support had the opposite effect. The tears she'd been holding inside at her frustration in not getting Nora back came pouring out of her in a torrent.

Honor felt as if her heart were bleeding.

She clung to Dakota, soaking his shoulder. All the while, he cradled her against his chest and rocked her. Should he let go, Honor knew she would sink to the floor in a weak-kneed puddle. Taking a deep breath, she fought for control, and by sheer will ended the waterworks.

"Feel better?" he asked, smoothing her hair.

"I w-won't feel better until I have my baby in my arms."

"All right, then, calmer?"

Starting to get embarrassed, she nodded and tried pushing herself away. Dakota's grip tightened and she furrowed her brow in silent question. He didn't speak, merely held her and searched her face with those perfect gemstone eyes. Honor's breath shortened, and she felt stirrings that would have held her captive without those arms to steady her.

He wasn't right for her—and yet, when his face drew closer, she didn't resist. She forgot about logic and led with her emotions.

Dakota's kiss was a burning promise, an assurance that everything would be all right, and Honor clung to that hope and to that kiss like a drowning woman in need of air. Then he drew her even closer, so that her thighs wedged between his and her breasts flattened against his chest.

Her thoughts changed dramatically as the flesh that lay atwixt caught fire, sent a message of such urgency surging through her that she forgot everything else. She pressed against him, took his tongue and played it with a sense of desperation. Her hands moved to his waist, found the edge of his T-shirt and slipped beneath the soft material. His flesh was warm and pliant and solid under her questing fingers.

Honor could hardly believe what was happening when Dakota withdrew and put some distance between them. She reached out to touch his cheek in an intimate appeal. He took her hand and softly kissed its palm.

"I don't understand," she whispered. From the way his eyes had darkened and his breathing had quickened, he was obviously aroused. "I need you."

"You need Nora. I'm convenient."

"No, that's not how—"

"It's all right. I understand."

But Honor didn't. She was tripped up by her own feelings, by what she wanted. Was it so very wrong, then, to yearn to be held and comforted when standing at the brink of despair? Perhaps not, a small voice inside her answered, but it would be wrong to use someone, and that's exactly what she would be doing if she made love with Dakota now. She would be using him to make herself feel better. She wasn't a woman who made love easily, and she didn't know this man well enough to care about him in that way.

She *didn't* care, did she?

In an attempt to cover her confusion and embarrassment, she pulled free of him, crossed to a living room window, stared out into the darkness and rationally analyzed the situation. Danger had drawn them together and danger had heightened both their senses. But that fragile bond was all that lay between them. Dakota had been correct to set her aside before they got carried away by something artificial.

"You don't have to wait with me," she said, carefully watching his reflection in the glass. "Who knows when I'll hear anything."

Expression intense, he stepped toward her, hands reaching as though he might take her in his arms once more. Then his hands dropped to his sides and his features softened, setting something inside her to yearning.

"I don't mind staying, Honor. You can kick me out if you don't want me here, but I'm in no hurry to leave. Maybe we could talk for a while, get to know each other better."

Distract me, Honor added silently, glad for the opportunity.

"Thanks. Why don't I get us some tea."

He didn't demur, so she set about making a pot of a soothing herbal mix that wouldn't make her jittery or keep her awake—not that she expected to sleep again until Nora was safe in her arms. A short while later, they were ensconced in the living room, Dakota on the sofa, she in the rocker, sipping the hot liquid, at first in silence, then sharing childhood memories, seemingly a safe topic.

"As an only child, I was pretty spoiled, I guess," Honor admitted. "And I was around actors a lot. Mom was personal assistant to Amanda Walsh," she said, referring to a glamour queen of the fifties.

"No wonder you wanted to become a movie star."

"After I was born, Mom took a job with a talent agency. That's actually how I got my big break."

"Your mother must have been delighted."

"She was. In a way, she invested all her hopes in me. I, uh, never knew my father, and Mom didn't remarry until I was making my first movie. Then she decided to be a housewife in North Carolina of all places."

"Is she happy?"

"Ecstatically."

"Then that's all that counts."

Honor added. "I should have learned from Mom's example, I guess, but I did miss having a father around while I was growing up. I guess that's why I wanted to believe in Gary so badly—so Nora could have the father I didn't. It just doesn't work that way... wishful thinking, I mean."

Not having a father around had probably made her stronger, more determined to succeed in any venture, and she wished the same for her daughter. Before she could immerse herself in thoughts that would bring her down again, Dakota asked, "So what kind of a little girl were you?"

Honor grinned. "According to Mom, I was a real hoyden from age four on."

"I can believe it. You remind me of Asia. She was a scrapper, never knew when to let something alone. She prided herself on being the toughest kid in the class."

"Tougher than the boys?"

"Way tougher!" Dakota boasted with a broad grin. "She was our mother's bane as well as her joy. I can't tell you the number of bloody noses I helped clean up so Mother wouldn't find out and be upset."

"Sounds as if you and Asia are close."

"We fought a lot—verbally, I mean—despite the age difference. She's six years younger than I am. But I guess you could say we're close."

"That's nice," Honor said, knowing how lonely being an only child could be. She didn't want that for Nora. Trying not to sink into a morass of longing and guilt, she said, "Sydney once told me you and she had a special bond, that you took care of her."

"Syd was always the sensitive one in the family," he said. "Whether it had to do with her mysterious premonitions or with our odd names."

"Dakota, Sydney, Asia—they are unusual."

"But of significance. Each of us was named for the place where we were conceived. Our parents traveled a lot, sometimes quite exotically, as evinced by my sister's names. I'm just a homespun kind of guy like Father. His name is Jasper, you know, as in Wyoming."

"Then it's a family tradition?" Honor smothered a giggle.

"What?"

"I was just imagining some of the bizarre names you could have been blessed with. Like Chicago. Or Albany."

"Or Moscow," Dakota added. "Kenya. Lima."

"How about Stockholm Raferty?" she suggested, laughing. "I'm sorry. I'm the last person in the world who should be making fun of someone else's name."

"If it'll keep you smiling, go ahead."

Reminded that she had no reason to smile, Honor sobered. Guilt that she'd once again forgotten about Nora, even if for only a few minutes, crept through her.

As if guessing her thoughts, Dakota gently commanded, "Honor, don't."

"I feel like I'm letting her down."

"You're not."

How could he say that after the way she'd tried to seduce him? "About what happened before . . ."

"Nothing happened that you need to worry about."

Honor was trying to figure out how to respond when the telephone rang. Heart thumping in her breast, she set down her teacup and flew to the telephone. Her hand trembled over the receiver.

Taking a deep breath, she picked it up with a grip that could cut off circulation and answered, "Hello?"

"Long time, no hear, huh?" came her ex-husband's voice. "What's up?"

"Gary."

She said it deliberately so Dakota would know. He nodded encouragingly.

"You sound surprised," her ex-husband was saying. "You're the one who left the message. I gathered you expected to hear from me."

"So you're home?" she asked, still looking at Dakota.

"Not exactly. I'm on location."

She shook her head and mouthed the word *no* before saying, "I thought you told me you just got back from location."

"Well, I'm gone again on a new assignment. You know how it is when you're good," Gary said, smoothly revving up to explain more than he might normally. "Roberta called and said they needed me pronto for an episode of *Houston.* I barely had time to throw a few things in a bag."

"So you're in Texas?" she said for Dakota's benefit.

Gary was beginning to sound a bit annoyed. "I thought I just established that."

"What hotel?"

"I'm on the move. Why don't you tell me why you called?" he asked, his good humor completely evaporating. "It isn't Nora, is it? Is she all right?"

Honor couldn't tell whether he was truly concerned or putting on an act. "I told her about your call. She just wanted to say hi to her Daddy."

"Oh." Was that relief Honor heard before he demanded, "Put my pumpkinhead on."

"She can't come to the phone," Honor said a little too quickly. She took a calming breath. "Nora's asleep."

"Again? Can't you wake her this time?"

"She's a little girl, Gary. She needs her rest."

Honor couldn't believe she was arguing, trying to sound convincing. If Gary had Nora, he would know better than she how their daughter fared. Under the circumstances, the conversation was ludicrous. She should be trying to figure out how to find him.

"Why don't you give me a number where I can reach you," she said. "We'll call in the morning."

"That's impossible," Gary insisted. "I'll call you."

"Gary, honey, will you be much longer?" Honor heard the woman's voice faint in the background. Gary quickly covered the receiver. Talking to his partner in crime? Or in bed? Honor wondered, no longer affected by her ex-husband's peccadilloes. More than likely both.

"Listen," Gary said, getting back to her. His voice was short now. "I've got to go. I'll call tomorrow."

Knowing she wasn't going to get anything further out of him, she didn't bother to object. "Sure, Gary, tomorrow," Honor muttered before hanging up.

"I take it he didn't tell you where he could be reached. That doesn't prove anything," Dakota pointed out.

"Doesn't it?"

"Don't indulge yourself in more wishful thinking," he said gently. "It'll just distract you from figuring out who the real criminals are."

"Wishful thinking?" she echoed, remembering that a short while before, she'd admitted to that very weakness in mistakenly trying to mold Gary into a fatherly role. "How can you be so sure that's all it is?"

And how could she be sure she wasn't fantasizing again, especially with Dakota giving her that look she could only interpret as pitying?

"You want desperately to believe Gary has Nora because, in your mind, that makes everything all right," Dakota stated. "You trust that he wouldn't hurt his own daughter. That's fine, I'm not going to disagree... *if* Gary is the one. Just don't fool yourself into complacency."

"Don't fool *yourself* into thinking I'm deluded where my ex-husband's concerned!" Honor returned hotly. "Gary may not be a vicious man—not even the criminal type—but he can be very childish, and a child makes up all kinds of excuses for bad behavior."

"So why would he want to implicate me?"

"You, as in personally?" Honor asked, eyebrows shooting up in surprise. "As you said before, he wouldn't even know who you were. The way I figure things, he needed help and paid for it by getting someone the information he wanted."

Dakota dismissed her theory with a careless shrug. "I've been giving the situation a lot of thought, as well. The sword could be double-edged. Not only might the mastermind behind this plot want to ruin my campaign against illegal fishing . . . but my whole career, as well."

"Now who's deluded?"

Dakota didn't bother to hide his annoyance. "If my integrity were questioned seriously, my public career could go down the tubes, Honor, and I'm not just talking about my lobbying activities."

He really was serious. "You mean your running for national office?"

"What do you think?"

She didn't know what to think where he was concerned—personally or professionally. But she was tired, too tired to keep up an argument that would get them nowhere.

"I think maybe you should go now."

"If that's what you want." His voice was tight. "But I won't back out of this, Honor. I'm going to do some investigating on my own."

"What kind of investigating?"

"I'll start by checking out Willard Zahniser. The old man never liked me much, and I'm becoming somewhat of a nasty thorn in his side. I wouldn't put it past him to try to pluck me out, no matter what it takes."

Knowing that Dakota could be correct, Honor didn't argue. He'd deflated her theory a bit, had given her more to worry about. But he wasn't at fault. He was only trying to help, she reminded herself. That he might be helping himself as much as her didn't matter. He'd gone the distance for her tonight, to which the bruises on his throat and jaw attested in living, putrid multicolors.

That he'd been unsuccessful didn't matter.

He'd tried his best, more than any man had ever done for her. Ever.

And so Honor showed Dakota to the door with a sense of unease that wouldn't be vanquished. He left without ceremony, without trying to touch her; she felt a sense of loss that was inexplicable. She moved to the window and stared out after him as he got in and started his car.

It wasn't until he pulled away from the curb, however, that another set of car lights flicked on.

And it wasn't until he stopped for the sign at the crossing and the other car hesitated halfway out of the parking spot that she thought anything of it.

When Dakota turned right and the other car did the same, Honor was certain of one thing: Dakota was being followed. And there was no way she could warn him!

DAKOTA WASN'T SURE EXACTLY when he became aware of the other car that stayed a short distance behind as he meandered across the downtown area. The car stayed equidistant, perhaps twenty or so yards back, even when Dakota stopped for a red light.

At this time of night, with so little traffic, he doubted the other driver's strange behavior was coincidence.

So he was being followed, assumably by someone waiting near Honor's place. But why? Did the kidnappers want to know where he was headed? Were they already aware that their quarry had turned on them? No, he doubted that they'd recognized him in jeans and an old T-shirt. His identity was undoubtedly the prize of the moment's game.

Adrenaline zipped through his veins . . . and the foot on the accelerator.

As the light turned green, his car shot out across the intersection while his eyes flicked to the rearview mirror. He smiled grimly when the other vehicle followed in like manner, as he knew it would.

Time to turn the tables.

Playing innocent, he slowed as though he didn't know he was being followed. He made several more turns, then, approaching a restaurant, he pulled over and pretended to park. The other car whizzed ahead.

And Dakota was directly behind. He hadn't been able to see a thing through the tinted windows of the dark Plymouth. Rather than lingering and following at a distance—no doubt the other driver was aware of his ploy anyway—Dakota stepped on the gas once more.

Closing the gap, he flicked on his brights and got a glimpse of a vanity license plate that read HOT something. The other car moved off so quickly, he was unable to get the rest.

Jaw clenched, determined to keep up with the other vehicle, Dakota did something that was an anathema to him. He broke the law to recklessly speed along near-deserted streets. The two cars zigzagged for blocks before heading first downhill toward the pier terminals, then north toward Queen Anne Hill.

And Dakota was doing a job of keeping up until motion flashed through his peripheral vision. He swerved and braked to avoid some jerk on a ten-speed determined to beat him across the intersection. His car bounced up over a curb, scraping the oil pan and who knew what else in the process before he was able to stop completely.

The biker gave him the high sign as he pedaled on.

And in the distance, a set of taillights seemed to mock his efforts as amateurish.

Dakota swore and carefully backed his car off the curb, hoping he hadn't done it any serious damage. Too late to go after the person who'd tailed him. But now his adrenaline was surging through him in a great rush. Too soon to go home to try to sleep.

Testing the car as he went—it seemed to have come through its near miss with flying colors—Dakota headed for his office. If nothing else, he could catch up on some paperwork he'd been putting off in favor of his work for Reynard Stirling.

The salmon-fishing industry was taking every waking moment of his time, invading every aspect of his life.

How could he not be personally involved when he knew the stakes? All his life, he'd wanted to emulate the man he most respected—his father. All his life, he'd wanted to make a contribution to society that equaled that of Judge Jasper Raferty.

Now everything was up for grabs.

The only positive in this crisis was meeting Honor. Though she'd gone about trying to save her daughter in the wrong way, he could understand it. In her panic, she'd made a mistake, one she now regretted. Honor was a woman worth knowing. She had so much love to give, was so loyal, so focused that he couldn't help but admire those traits in her.

Now that she was on the ethical track, he was having a difficult time resisting her other qualities. Her looks and sex appeal had never been in question, and her personality shone through all but her darkest moments.

Entering his office, Dakota knew he had to banish Honor Bright from his mind for a while if he was to get anything accomplished. He sat down to work. He became so absorbed in trying to knock out the paperwork he'd been letting go that he didn't hear the elevator until it clunked to a stop on his floor. Reacting, he turned off his light and rushed into the outer office, where he did the same just as the elevator doors slid open.

A feeling of foolishness suddenly washed over him— no doubt it was only Grady making his rounds. But the heels clacking down the hall belonged to no man. Hand over the light switch, Dakota tensed as a key scraped the lock.

Chapter Eight

Don't let it be Honor, he thought silently.

The second the door swung open, Dakota flicked on the light and was taken aback by the sight of the woman who jumped and gasped in shock.

"What the hell are you doing here?" he demanded.

Janet Ingel put a hand to her throat and pulled in a ragged breath of air. Her eyes were wide, as if she'd seen a ghost. "My God, you gave me a scare!"

"So what are you doing here?" he reiterated, frowning at her.

"The same as you...I suppose. I've got some work to catch up on."

"After midnight?"

"Late date. Have a problem with that? I didn't want the guy to take me home, so I had him leave me off here." Now Janet was frowning in return, not to mention closely eyeing his unusual attire. "Why are you questioning me like I've done something wrong?"

"Sorry." Dakota knew very well that ambitious Janet often worked extra hours. "I didn't expect company."

"Neither did I. If you'll excuse me..."

Janet stalked off to her office while Dakota returned to his. He got back to work. After a few distracted minutes, he rose and crossed to her doorway, where he leaned against the jamb and cleared his throat.

"Janet, sorry if I scared you."

Brow furrowed, she looked up at him. "It's all right. I guess I would have been just as spooked if I'd have been here alone."

Dakota nodded and started to go.

"Wait a minute." When he turned back, she said, "I owe you an apology, as well. I shouldn't have gotten on your case this morning. I should have realized you would be fair in making your decision about taking on Safehouses. Sometimes I get . . . too intense."

"I've already forgotten about it."

"Listen. I—I'd like to make it up to you. I know you're swamped. Can I help?"

Though members of the cooperative often helped one another in an emergency, this was the first time Janet had extended her hand to him. Dakota thought it would be wise to take her up on the offer.

"I'm taking care of some odds-and-ends paper-work. The salmon-fishing industry is my focus right now. Are you interested in getting involved?"

"I'll be happy to do whatever I can. Why don't you give me a look at the background materials."

Dakota hesitated at the mention of the infamous file. Then he relaxed. "I have a better idea. I'm going to set up an appointment over at NCSC tomorrow morning. Maybe you can come with me, get a feel for the problem firsthand."

"Sure. If I'm available." She paused a second, then asked, "What happened to you, anyway?" She indicated the bruising.

"Stupidity on my part," he lied. "I tripped on some clothes I left on the floor of my loft bedroom. I hit the railing."

"Ooh, looks painful." With a polite smile that indicated end-of-conversation, Janet went back to her work.

Dakota attempted to get his mind on his own backlog, but found that his thoughts kept straying to the anticipated meeting with Zahniser. Finally, he packed up and left for home.

A few minutes later, he parked the car on his street off Pioneer Square. As he headed for his building, he had the strangest feeling. He stopped and looked around but saw no watching eyes. Only as he opened the vestibule door did he see the reflection of what appeared to be the dark Plymouth that had followed him to Honor's place. Before he could turn, the vehicle sped around the corner and was gone.

If his identity had been the purpose of the pursuit, mission accomplished. All the driver had to do was return and check the half dozen names listed next to the bells.

Wearily, Dakota trudged up the stairs. His phone started to ring before he even had the key in the lock. Honor. Who else would be calling him in the middle of the night? Hopefully, she'd heard about Nora, perhaps even had her daughter safe and sound. The door was open by the third ring. He answered by the fourth.

"Thank God you're all right!" she cried. "Where have you been? I was so worried. I've been calling every ten minutes for the past hour."

"I'm flattered. I stopped at the office after being detoured."

"You knew you were being followed, then?" She sighed. "I was so worried you wouldn't notice, that something would happen to you."

"I'm fine. What about you?"

A moment's pause. Then she answered, "I've been better."

"I was hoping you might have heard from them."

"Not as much as I was."

"Try to get some sleep," he suggested.

"Every time I close my eyes, I see her...." Voice choked with emotion, her words trailed off.

Dakota wished he had stayed to give Honor the support she so desperately needed. As unfathomable as it seemed to him, he was more worried about her than was appropriate, considering how long they'd known each other. He was getting caught up in a stranger's life—and he wasn't sure that was wise.

"Try heating up some milk," he suggested. "Syd swears that when stress gets to her, nothing relaxes her and lets her sleep like a glass of warm milk."

"Maybe I'll try that," Honor said, but Dakota didn't think she sounded convinced.

They talked for a few more minutes. Dakota didn't rush her. He gave her what comfort he could though he was dead on his feet. Still, no matter how many assurances he made, he could hear the ever-present fear in her voice. And when they finally said good-night, he was the one who had trouble sleeping.

Every time he closed his eyes he saw her....

WARM MILK HADN'T WORKED worth a damn. Unable to settle down to rest, no less sleep, Honor had tossed and turned for hours before deciding to take action. She couldn't leave Nora's safety to fate or to the kidnappers or even to Dakota. She had to do something herself.

"A little late this morning, aren't you?" the guard asked as he let her in the back entrance of her own office building at quarter past six.

Bobbing her babushka-covered head and shrugging her plaid-shirted shoulders, Honor said, "Late, mister, sorry," in her best imitation of a Polish accent.

As she hurried down the hall, the guard clucked and went back to his morning newspaper and coffee.

Honor had been pretty sure she would get into the building without his questioning her. New cleaning people came and went, sometimes only after a few weeks. He couldn't know every member of the janitorial staff. She'd been counting on that fact to fool him.

And the makeup job she'd done on her face would hide her identity from anyone else who might see her. She'd added ten years to her age by changing the texture of her skin and adding tiny crows' feet around her eyes and mouth. Her eyebrows were now dark brown rather than auburn, and there were bluish circles under her eyes.

No one would pay her any mind—except, perhaps, the supervisor. Honor would be sure to stay out of sight of the eagle-eyed second-floor overseer.

After what she'd gone through to get into Dakota's

office, getting into Zahniser's was going to be a piece of cake. While sometime that morning Dakota would wage a frontal assault, Honor was afraid he wouldn't learn anything of value more than having his suspicions confirmed. That wasn't enough. And that's why she was going to attack from the rear, before Zahniser was alerted.

A man mopping the hall looked over his shoulder as she treaded on his wet floor. "Hey, I just cleaned that!" he yelled at her.

"Sorry, mister!" she called back, waving at him as she opened the nearest stairwell door.

She practically ran all the way up to the next floor, hoping against hope that the guy wouldn't alert anyone. Now that was paranoid thinking, Honor told herself, taking a deep breath before exiting into the second-floor hallway.

No one in sight.

Relieved, she set off for the nearest janitor's closet and found a basket filled with cleaning supplies. So far, so good. If only her luck would hold. All she needed was to run into the person who really was supposed to be cleaning Zahniser's offices. The hallway floor here looked as if it had already been mopped. The drone of a vacuum came from some office in the opposite direction, and another upright vacuum cleaner stood sentinel at the executive-suite doorway.

Honor approached cautiously, noting she wouldn't have to use her own key that would unlock the outer door. It stood open, but there didn't seem to be anyone around. Break time so early in the morning?

Sliding into the suite, she quietly closed and locked the door behind her and set her cleaning supplies on a low vertical file near the receptionist's desk. Now, to get into Zahniser's private office. More than once, she'd seen Joan take a master set of keys out of the middle desk drawer. She prayed the receptionist was a creature of habit.

And she prayed her own desk key would open Joan's, which was identical to hers.

It did.

But when she slid the middle drawer with difficulty—for some reason it was sticking—no keys were there to meet her gaze. Quickly searching through the side drawers, she found nothing. She was about to start over when she heard footsteps approaching.

Adrenaline shot through her system as her sense of self-preservation was alerted. Now what? The footsteps stopped at the executive-suite door and the doorknob jiggled. She was sure she heard cursing in some foreign language. Her pulse began to throb.

She had to hide. But where?

Honor did the first thing that occurred to her—she ducked under the desk, sat on the floor with her knees to her chin and pulled the chair into the recess as cover.

And just in time.

No sooner had she gotten herself into position than the person unlocked the door and opened it. Whoever entered continued talking to herself and dragged the vacuum into the room. Honor was wondering if she could be seen past the chair when her gaze froze on the cleaning supplies she'd left on the vertical file.

Nerves tingled along her spine. What if the cleaning woman saw the basket? What if she were discovered?

She should have brazened it out rather than hidden like a coward. That was what her disguise had been for, after all. Now she was stuck . . . like a sitting duck.

The vacuum roared to life, swept back and forth, came ever closer, inch-by-inch, its obnoxious whine making her cover her ears. She waited for it to circle the desk, for the chair to slide out, for the woman to shriek in surprise. When the machine's edge sneaked under the desk edge and hit her in the hip, Honor jumped and smashed her head into the bottom of the middle drawer. The vacuum stopped suddenly to be replaced by a rattling noise directly overhead.

Barely a foot away, the other woman stood still, no doubt listening!

Frozen in fear, Honor began to sweat.

If she were discovered now, it would all be over! She wouldn't get a look at Zahniser's office—and, if he were indeed mixed up in this plot, he would be warned that they were on to him. That wouldn't bode well for Nora. In the meantime, she would have to make a run for it, get past both the cleaning people and the guard. Would she be able to get away, identity intact, yet again?

Muscles coiled, head spinning as she tried to formulate a plan of escape, she awaited discovery.

"Aren't you through in here yet?" came a strident voice from the hall.

The cleaning woman shifted from her frozen position. "Through, yes."

"Then get yerself outta here and start on the next office. We don't have all day, you know."

Muttering, the woman dragged her vacuum back to the hall.

As the door shut with a bang, Honor whispered, "Good old Eunice." The second floor supervisor had unwittingly saved her butt.

Once out of her hiding place, Honor lost no time in trying the middle drawer again. Rather than merely sticking a little as it had the first time, the drawer dragged and made a screeching metallic sound that zipped down Honor's spine as she fought to open it. And what if someone in the hall heard? Impatient and becoming a little desperate, she gave the handle a determined jerk. With another rattle and clunk, whatever had been caught freed itself and landed on the floor under the desk.

The keys! Joan must have thrown them all the way to the back of the drawer. When Honor had bumped her head, she must have lodged them further between drawer and desk top.

Grabbing the ring, worried that someone might yet come back, she hastily set things right. The cleaning basket came with her as she made her way to the short hall in front of Zahniser's office. She tried key after key, only managing to find the correct one after a half dozen tries.

The click of the door opening signaled the start of what could be a gargantuan task. Checking her watch, Honor took a deep breath. She figured she had barely an hour to find what she could and escape unscathed. Not enough time, but it would have to do.

Honor feared Nora's safety depended on her success.

SEVEN IN THE MORNING WAS early for a visit, but King Crawley had taken pleasure in breaking rules since he was a green kid. And now that he was at the other end of the spectrum, he paid well enough to do what he wanted—when he wanted.

Sitting at the scarred table, he looked over the contents of the new delivery with interest. "This is more like it."

"Then you have what you need?" The question was filled with the sound of relief.

"Mmm. I'm not certain this is enough." Even if it were, he might not let his visitor off the hook so easily. "I'll let you know after I have it checked out."

"The situation is becoming too unhealthy. If you haven't heard yet, the Bright woman has help."

"Who?"

"Dakota Raferty himself."

"Ah, the game is gonna get interesting," Crawley said with a sense of satisfaction he'd feared he might never have, despite his machinations. "A few bonus points. Raferty can watch helplessly as his career—maybe his whole life, if I'm real lucky—is flushed down the head."

"He's anything but helpless." A short pause was followed by, "He can be dangerous."

When it came down to it, Crawley thought, his visitor was more bluff than backbone. Promises to do whatever was necessary made in the beginning had turned out to be so much talk. But Crawley meant to push it, to get every drop of blood he could for his favors.

That was, after all, what he did best.

"But Raferty's not as dangerous as I am, right?" he finally commented.

The implied threat worked.

And Crawley suspected his friend wished they'd never been introduced.

"BEING ON OPPOSING SIDES of an issue doesn't mean we can't be friends," Willard Zahniser told Dakota later that morning, when he and Janet arrived. He took a close look at Dakota's neck but didn't say a word. Dakota had concealed the bruises on his throat as best he could with makeup.

Dakota had insisted on the meeting over the CEO's protests, and now Zahniser was playing with him. Or would be, if Dakota weren't too smart to fall for the bull. Shaking the CEO's hand, he returned the man's smile without responding to the ludicrous suggestion. Zahniser didn't want Dakota for a friend any more than he wanted this meeting.

Andrew Vaughn took the cigar out of his mouth long enough to say, "Yeah, we can be real buddies, right Raferty?"

"Think so?" Dakota was sure Vaughn knew he was the last person in the world anyone with any ethics would associate with.

"Actually, I'd rather be chummy with the babe."

Vaughn leered at Janet, who merely raised her dark eyebrows and primly took her seat at the conference table. "I don't see any babes here," she said smartly.

Dakota was glad to see Janet wasn't at a loss for words. But then, why should she be, considering her background. Vaughn was probably a pussycat compared to some of the men Janet had handled during her years growing up in poverty-stricken, gang-ridden neighborhoods. And while new in the arena, she was already proving herself as a worthy lobbying opponent.

The men sat and Zahniser got right down to business. "So, what can we do for you?"

"We both have a great deal of time and money invested in our lobbying efforts connected with the salmon-fishing industry," Dakota said. "I thought we could make life easier for everyone if we put our cards on the table."

Expecting Vaughn to make some crack, Dakota was surprised when the man sat silently puffing on his cigar. He didn't even give Janet a second glance after his initial come-on. As a matter of fact, he seemed to be somewhat removed, as if his mind were elsewhere.

"What kind of cards?" the CEO asked, the smile never slipping from his lips.

"Say our mutual interest in overfishing by certain large Seattle-based companies." Dakota didn't intimate this was a situation Zahniser condoned, since that wouldn't accomplish anything.

"Overfishing? That's a problem that keeps cropping up. I don't happen to have any facts or figures."

"Reynard Stirling does," Dakota responded casually.

A glimmer of uncertainty passed through Zahniser's eyes behind his thick lenses. He recovered gracefully and assumed an air of innocence when he asked, "I imagine he has shared these facts and figures with you?"

"Most certainly."

"So? You're here to threaten me?" he questioned, his tone not changing a bit. He was sounding too reasonable for the implications. "I run an organization that promotes a product. I have nothing to do with over-fishing.''

"You represent the companies that do," Janet said, intimating guilt by association.

A moment of tension telegraphed from Zahniser before he laughed. "That's rich." He shook his head and seemed almost jovial. "PILC has always been noted for cradle snatching." His gaze snagged Dakota's, eliminating Janet from the conversation. "You really ought to make sure you train your kids before setting them loose on the big boys."

Janet choked out, "Now wait a minute—"

Dakota touched her arm and firmly said, "Let's all hold it a second. We're getting off the topic. What Miss Ingel meant was that if some companies are running a scam operation, it hurts all the ones who don't. And if we get our way...it'll hurt others unless they get smart."

Feigning only mild interest, Zahniser stretched back in his chair and asked, "What do you mean?"

"We're going to make it tough on anyone who deals with companies that sell illegal catches."

"You'd have to prove intent."

"Would we?"

Dakota didn't push. He merely enjoyed watching Zahniser as the man tried to hide his reaction to the threat. He was successful if not quick enough. Normally, he would have blasted Dakota right out of the room, but today, he didn't even try. And Vaughn remained unnaturally quiet—bored, even, as if the salmon-fishing industry weren't part of his life's blood.

Something was going on here, Dakota decided. Both men were acting totally out of character. One, if not both, was involved—of that he was certain.

FRUSTRATION FILLED EVERY pore of Honor's being as she entered the lobby of the building holding the NCSC offices—this time dressed as herself.

Her morning playing detective had been a total bust as far as she was concerned. She had nothing but several company names that might or might not be of help. She could have been looking directly at the evidence that would incriminate Zahniser and not have recognized it. As far as she could tell, she'd found nothing to implicate the man.

Nothing!

And she still hadn't gotten another call from the kidnappers. Did any mother whose child was missing ever get used to the waiting?

Looking over her shoulder as if she might catch someone following her, too late, she heard the doors of the elevator slide open. Knocked off balance, she turned and stared directly at Dakota. She had a quick impression of Janet Ingel and Andrew Vaughn directly behind him. Without thinking, she feigned clumsiness and dropped her purse.

Items scattered across the floor the way they had the last time she saw Nora.

Unready for the emotions that would stir in her at the reminder, Honor blinked and stared. "Sorry," she choked out, flashing her gaze significantly to Ingel and Vaughn. She thought it unwise to reveal her friendly relationship with Dakota to anyone working for NCSC—especially Vaughn—and hoped Dakota would understand.

He got the message. "No problem, miss. Here, let me help you." Stooping, he glanced at his coworker over his shoulder. "Janet, I'll be with you in a minute."

Honor thought the dark-haired woman was going to give them away, but she covered her surprised expression as Dakota started gathering Honor's things. Vaughn gave her a searching look, then turned his attention to the other woman.

"I'll keep the novice here entertained," Vaughn said, trying to steer Janet out of the lobby's light midmorning pedestrian traffic. "She and I have a few things to chew on anyway, don't we, babe?"

"Get your hands off of me," Janet said through gritted teeth, pulling her arm from his grasp. "And we have nothing whatsoever to discuss."

Puffing on his cigar through gritted teeth, he insisted, "Oh, I think we do...."

Whether or not she agreed, Janet swept by Vaughn in the direction he'd been indicating.

Honor stooped near Dakota, though he had things in hand. "How did the meeting go?" she asked softly.

"Both Zahniser and Vaughn may be involved. Nothing concrete, just a feeling that something wasn't right," he admitted, stuffing her wallet and checkbook into the clutch. "It could have gone better."

She grabbed a lipstick and dropped it inside. "Then you weren't any more successful than I was."

"You? What are you talking about?"

"I couldn't sleep," she said, rising. "So I pretended to be part of the janitorial staff this morning. I searched Zahniser's office."

"You what?"

Dakota popped up and grabbed her elbow. He pulled her away from the elevators—and as faraway as possible from the two lobbyists, who were clearly arguing about some issue or other.

"What the hell did you think you were doing?" he snarled in a lowered voice.

Anger overwhelming her, Honor whispered with equal force. "Trying to do something positive! Nora is my daughter."

"But if you had been caught . . ."

Realizing worry tempered his words, Honor let go of the breath she was holding. "Why are we arguing when we're on the same side?"

"You're right. I just . . ."

His voice trailed off yet again as he smoothed a curl from her forehead. At his gentle touch, something in Honor broke. She hated playing games, hated pretending she didn't even know Dakota when she yearned for his touch, wanted to be held by him, needed to be in his arms.

Dakota had gotten to her on a very primal level—not just physically, but emotionally, as well—and she didn't know what she was going to do about it. Suddenly, his being a lobbyist didn't seem to bother her. He was nothing like Andrew Vaughn; her thinking so had been an excuse to push him away. And the fact that he hadn't immediately given her the file to trade for Nora paled in light of all that he *had* done since.

Brushing her cheek, he dropped his hand. As if of their own accord, her fingers found his and twined with them. In the moment of connected silence, she tried to convey all she was feeling through her eyes.

"Well, well, isn't this a touching scene?"

Guiltily pulling back her hand, Honor whipped around to face Karen Lopinski. The bulldog of a reporter was standing a yard away, her smirk big enough to make Honor want to slap it off her face. Despite that, she kept her control and feigned innocence, but she wasn't fooling anyone. The knowing look in Lopinski's eyes didn't bode well.

"Excuse me, but this is a private conversation," Honor said.

"I'll just bet it is."

"Look, Lopinski—"

"Don't bother to deny anything, Raferty. You only make yourself sound foolish." The reporter chuckled. "You *look* foolish, too."

She was staring at the clutch in Dakota's hand, which he promptly offered to Honor.

As the purse exchanged hands, Lopinski affected an evil little grin. "Don't be surprised when I get the goods on you two. You're going to make a hot story yet." Her gaze swept the lobby and stopped when it got to Vaughn and Janet, who were still arguing. "But not today. Looks like I've got bigger fish to fry. Ta."

The reporter made a beeline to corner the two lobbyists, undoubtedly thinking she could get the scoop on whatever hot issue they were debating.

"Sorry about that," Dakota said.

"I'm probably more used to her kind than you are." Now that she had the bag in hand, Honor reopened it and unzippered an inner compartment. "When I was going through Zahniser's office, I found mention of contributions to NCSC. I recognized some of the company names from the files you showed me. I didn't know if it was important or not, so I copied them down for you."

She pulled out the list, and with a furtive look over her shoulder to make sure the reporter was still busy with the lobbyists, she slipped the folded paper to Dakota, who equally covertly slid the list into his own pocket.

"I'll go over it later," he said.

"I doubt that it's anything, but you never know."

"I'd better get going before Vaughn gets suspicious," Dakota said, glancing toward the lobbyist, who was going on about something to the reporter. "I'll see you later."

As he strode off, Honor echoed, "Later." She would cling to the one bright spot she had to look forward to and could only hope they would have reason to celebrate.

DAKOTA ARRIVED AT JANET'S side just seconds after Karen Lopinski took off for the elevators, pursuing Honor once again. Nothing he could do about that.

"Ready to leave?" he asked his coworker.

"Not quite," she said, surprising him. Her voice was as strained as her expression. "You go ahead. I'll meet you back at the office."

Vaughn took the cigar out of his mouth. "Yeah, the babe and me aren't through."

If Dakota expected Janet to deny that, he was disappointed. She merely clenched her jaw and forced a smile for him. Wondering what the argument was all about, he left, reluctant but certain Janet would fill him in later. With a last glance at the elevators—he frowned when he saw Lopinski follow Honor into an empty car—he left the building.

What did Lopinski want? What kind of havoc would she wreak this time?

Thinking that buying a copy of the rag she worked for would be a wise move, he crossed the street to a newsstand tucked into a tiny first-floor space with a window on the sidewalk.

"*Northwest Eye,*" he told the vendor, handing the man a dollar.

Dakota quickly scanned the front page. He was relieved when he saw no pictures of him or Honor splattered there as he had feared. No story, either. He opened the rag and carefully scanned a page at a time to make sure the story—whatever it might be—wasn't buried.

Nothing.

The only article with Lopinski's byline was a story about the growing homeless population in Seattle—sensationalized, as usual.

With a sense of relief that she wasn't on his back yet, he pitched the newspaper into a trash can. About to leave for his own office, he glanced toward the NCSC building just in case Janet was finished, as well.

She wasn't the one he spotted. She wasn't the one who rooted his feet to the cement walk.

Lester Freidman was entering the building. Dakota would have recognized the erstwhile accountant anywhere after the Crawley trial. As far as he knew, Freidman still worked for King Crawley, though the Seattle racketeer had been incarcerated for a couple of years now.

As far as Dakota knew, the Crawley organization didn't have any fingers in the salmon-fishing pie, so what was King Crawley's right-hand man doing at NCSC?

Chapter Nine

Dakota was still wondering about Freidman, among others, when he arrived at his office.

"Is Janet back?" he asked Lori, one of the clerks, thinking the other lobbyist might have left NCSC without his noticing while he was skimming the *Northwest Eye*.

"I thought she was with you."

"Was," Dakota agreed. "When she comes in, tell her I'm looking for her."

"Sure thing."

The way Janet and Vaughn had been arguing, Dakota wanted to find out what the sleazeball had been up to.

In the meantime, he thought, entering his office and closing the door behind him, he had some serious thinking to do about Freidman. Anything that had to do with the Crawley organization made him feel a little dizzy...not to mention sick to his stomach.

The racketeer's trial had thrust Dakota into the limelight—and onto the front page of the *Northwest Eye*—when Maureen had gone to work for McCarthy,

Donnelly and Strong, the lawfirm representing Crawley.

Staring out the window, Dakota remembered how Karen Lopinski had gotten wind of the story before anyone else. The only reason she'd been scooped had been the immediacy of the electronic media. But that hadn't stopped Lopinski. She'd gone after him with a vengeance, as though her reason for trying to ruin him were personal.

But that was ridiculous, wasn't it?

Dakota couldn't think of a thing the reporter might have against him.

Whatever her reason, the result of Lopinski's particularly vicious attack had been a smear campaign that had made him withdraw from the upcoming election. Knowing he'd lost the confidence of many of his constituents, he'd pulled out and switched gears.

Lobbying had seemed a safe avenue for someone who wanted to work in the public interest but who had a small scandal—albeit not of his own making—hanging over his head. Now he feared the persecution would start all over again, not only killing his chances for national office, but rendering him ineffective as a lobbyist, as well.

Vengeance? he wondered. Or unthinking, career-driven selfishness?

Feeling as if he were shooting arrows at a nonexistent target, Dakota decided to do something he could get a handle on—like take a look at the list of companies making contributions to NCSC. He pulled the sheet of paper from his pocket and unfolded it. He recognized most of the company names listed. Only three were unfamiliar to him.

He placed a quick call to Reynard Stirling.

"Ever hear of Blueback Hatcheries, Kingfish Entitlements or Pacifico, Inc.?" Dakota asked.

"Blueback Hatcheries is a new company," Reynard told him. "Small, aggressive. I'm acquainted with the owners, who seem to be upright citizens. Never heard of the other two. You have something on them?"

"No, I was hoping you could tell me. You remember the problem I warned you about?" Without waiting for a confirmation, he explained, "One of these companies may be involved."

"Hmm. I'll get my man on it. The end of the day soon enough?"

"I knew I could count on you."

"Just as I count on you to do some explaining—"

"Soon," Dakota interrupted. "I hope to God it'll be soon."

For Honor's sake as well as his own.

That done, he sat back and thoughtfully went over his options. He couldn't keep his mind on work, and he couldn't sit there all day pretending. Honor and Nora and his own career were uppermost in his mind. He had to act. And he knew exactly how he was going to proceed.

As he locked his door, he noticed Janet was engrossed in some papers on her desk. He stepped over to her office and knocked on the jamb.

She jumped, and her face flamed. "Oh, Dakota."

"Didn't Lori tell you I was looking for you?"

"I'm sorry. I wanted to make a quick call before we talked. I got involved . . . and then I forgot," she finished lamely. "You want to discuss the meeting this morning?"

"Not much to discuss." From the flush on her face, he doubted that she'd forgotten anything. He'd swear she was trying to avoid him. "I was more curious about what Vaughn wanted."

The flush grew deeper as she said, "Nothing."

"But you were arguing. Come on, Janet, give. Was he giving you a hard time in general, or did he have something more specific in mind?"

She was looking in his direction, but not at him. Her mind seemed preoccupied with other things.

"He, uh, was coming on to me. He didn't want to take no for an answer."

Dakota could tell she didn't want to say more on the subject. He backed off, even though he wasn't at all certain she was telling the truth. Not that he had any other reason to suspect otherwise. Call it instinct.

"Well, so much for the inside track," he said. "See you tomorrow."

"You're not coming back after lunch?" she asked, obviously startled.

"Can't I play hooky for once?"

"Sure, why not? You just didn't seem the type. Going any place special?"

Odd that she'd even ask. "Home," he lied. "Thought I'd catch up on some reading."

Her eyebrows arched, but she didn't say anything more, merely went back to her work.

Dakota left the office wondering about her interest and about the real reason for the argument she'd had with Vaughn. The two lobbyists had been practically nose to nose about something. If it had been a blatant pass, Janet would have frosted the sleazeball over. Heading toward his destination, however, Dakota soon put Janet out of mind as memories of another dark-haired woman crowded his thoughts.

He remembered a lot of things over a quick lunch, which he wolfed down at a small restaurant on the way.

And, a half hour later, as he entered the building that housed McCarthy, Donnelly and Strong, he steeled himself against any lingering emotions he might still have for Maureen O'Neil. But when he was escorted into her office and he saw his ex-fiancée for the first time in more than two years, Dakota realized he no longer felt a thing.

Maureen rose, a tentative smile playing around her lips. "Dakota, your coming to see me is such a surprise."

"It surprised me, too."

The door wooshed closed behind him as the secretary discreetly left. Maureen stood. Dakota stared, surprised that her beauty had no effect on him at all. An image of Honor flashed through his mind, and he wondered how much the actress had to do with his forgetting about the woman he'd once loved so desperately.

As if catching herself doing something forbidden, Maureen suddenly shook her head. "Is this visit professional . . . or personal?"

He couldn't believe he actually saw a flicker of hope crossing her classic features. Now *that* had some effect. It bothered him.

"Let's say a little of both."

"Please, sit down."

Dakota sat in the black leather chair opposite hers and took a good look around the room, starting with Maureen's sleek black Eurostyle desk. The office was modern and luxurious. Track lighting washed abstracts hung on the walls. This space was the antithesis of the hole-in-the-wall that had been hers as a public defender. Everything had that designer touch...including Maureen herself. Today she wore a pearl-gray suit and pale blue blouse that set off her cloud of perfectly coiffed shoulder-length dark hair and gray-blue eyes.

Those eyes were staring at him, waiting for him to state his case. An old lawyer's trick he recognized, though it had been more than a decade since he'd practiced law. She, of course, wanted the upper hand. Dakota wasn't willing to give it to her any sooner than necessary. He knew better than to state his purpose until he had her a little flustered—assuming he could still manage it.

"You've got quite a setup for yourself here," he observed. "I guess you knew what you were doing when you decided to make your move and damn the personal cost."

A twinge of discomfort tightened her features. "A woman has to take her opportunities where she can."

"And not look back?"

"I looked back." Maureen sighed and asked, "Is that why you're here, to dredge up old news? Or is it possible you want a new start—"

Dakota interrupted before she could embarrass herself too badly. "What I want is a favor. Are you up to doing one for an old . . . friend?"

Caution shaded her eyes and she sat back, withdrawing emotionally as well as physically. "That depends."

"I won't ask for anything I couldn't get another way. Coming to you is merely expedient. Your telling me what I need to know will simplify my life at the moment."

"Yes. I remember how simple things were for you," she said, bitterness creeping into the words. "Black or white, right or wrong. No in-between."

Dakota ignored the familiar criticism and went straight to his purpose. "What link does King Crawley's organization have to the Northwest Coast Salmon Council?"

"Link? I don't know what you're talking about. As for Crawley, he's not running any organization from prison. How could he?"

Maureen had donned her lawyer's face. Inscrutable. Sharp. Dakota thought if anyone could break through, he could.

"Let's not play games. I saw Lester Freidman at the NCSC building this morning."

"And you think I should know what some accountant was doing there."

"I'd say you could make an educated guess. This particular accountant was—and is—Crawley's right-hand man, and we both know it." Dakota played her game for a minute and stared. When he sensed she was getting uncomfortable, he added, "You owe me at least this much, Maureen."

She flinched and dropped her gaze. "All right, I'm sure you could find out through other sources. Crawley has made some heavy contributions to NCSC."

He fingered the pocket that held the list of contributors. "Why?"

"Now that I can't tell you." Before he could object, she held out her hand to stay him. "I'm not holding back. I honestly don't know. No one has confided in me, and I'm not a mind reader. Why are you interested?"

"Call it curiosity."

"Dakota—"

Whatever Maureen was about to say was interrupted by the telephone ringing. Reluctantly, she picked up the receiver and hit a button.

"Yes." She listened for a second. "Right this minute? Can't it wait?"

Her gaze connected with Dakota's once more and in it, he read regret—or as close to that emotion as Maureen was capable of feeling.

"All right." Hanging up, she said, "This will only take a minute. Wait for me. Please."

Dakota neither answered nor got up to leave. But the moment the door closed behind Maureen, he was at her desk, opening the Rollodex and searching for a notepad and pencil. He flipped to *F* and found the card that held Freidman's address and telephone number. He quickly copied the information.

And then, before Maureen could return and possibly embarrass him or herself, he left her office without looking back.

The memory of how she had betrayed him had held him emotional prisoner since their breakup. But all that had changed in a few days. He didn't know how this could be happening to a man who'd gotten to rely on easy relationships, but since he'd met her, only one woman interested him, filled his thoughts day and night.

Dakota faced the facts: he was falling in love with Honor Bright.

HONOR STARED AT THE salmon-colored walls. What was she still doing in her office? It wasn't as if she had work to do. Her schedule was normally light, and today's was no exception. NCSC required her presence at meetings and public appearances, and she made an occasional commercial. The office was merely window dressing, a place to hang her hat, so to speak, or a place to give interviews. Nothing more.

Today she had no meetings, no appearances, no interviews. So what was she doing here?

She couldn't go home. That was the problem. She couldn't stand the emptiness, the reminder of Nora's absence. Dear God, how long could she survive her daughter's loss without going crazy? Being alone was draining the sanity from her. She needed to be with someone who understood, someone she could talk to.

That someone was Dakota Raferty.

Unable to get the thought out of her mind, she picked up her phone and punched out his office number. He'd gone for the day, so she called him at home. His machine answered. She didn't bother to leave a message.

Then she dialed her own number for the hundredth time since she'd arrived, hoping against hope that the kidnappers had finally called. She brightened when she heard Dakota's voice.

"Hi, it's me. I'm on my way home, but I don't know how long I'll be there. I got a lead I plan on following up as soon as possible. Keep your fingers crossed. I'll call you sometime tonight."

A beep was followed by silence. The kidnappers hadn't called.

Swallowing her disappointment at that, she replaced the receiver in the cradle and concentrated on the lead

Dakota had. Maybe this was it! Maybe whatever he'd learned would lead them straight to her child.

The instant she closed her eyes, Honor could see Nora, her copper braids about to come unfurled, a streak of grime on her little nose as she worked in the garden, getting as much dirt on herself as she did around the plants. The little girl seemed so very serious, so intent and proud of *her* garden, which mimicked her mother's.

The memory made Honor smile despite the tears that threatened her eyes.

Taking a shaky breath, she made her decision to leave now, to try to catch Dakota at home. She'd wait if she had to. What else did she have to do with her time? Whatever his lead was, she would follow it up with him. They were a team.

And once they were together, her situation wouldn't seem so hopeless. He gave her confidence, filled her with faith, made her believe in relationships again. Dakota was a man she could count on.

Remembering how he'd put her off when she'd wanted some physical comfort the day before, Honor only hoped she wasn't counting on too much.

"MY P.I. GOT THE INFORMATION you needed," Reynard said, when Dakota answered his home phone. "Pacifico, Inc. distributes professional fishing equipment, but Kingfish Entitlements is a little more slippery."

Already anticipating the answer, Dakota asked, "What did you find out?"

Satisfaction was ripe in Reynard's tone as he said, "Kingfish Entitlements is a subsidiary of a subsidiary of a company owned by—"

"King Crawley," Dakota finished for him.

"Nice guess!"

An easy one after having talked to Maureen, Dakota thought. "So what *is* Kingfish Entitlements?"

"I wish I could tell you. It's kind of a mystery company, all on paper from what we can tell, though my man says there are rumors of dock workers' union involvement."

"Sounds like Crawley."

"If I knew more about—"

"Can't do it, Reynard, not just yet. But I think I'm getting close."

"Good thing I'm a patient man."

Dakota was suitably grateful. Though he knew he could trust Reynard Stirling with his or anyone else's life, Nora wasn't his child. He rapidly brought the conversation to a close and tried the number for Lester Freidman.

No answer, not even a machine. Now what?

He planned to pay the accountant a visit. That he might be better off searching the man's home while it stood empty occurred to him, but straight arrow that he was, Dakota immediately discounted the idea. No, he would face Freidman man-to-man and try to get information by pressure tactics. He wasn't ready to sink to the crook's level yet . . . if ever.

So he would wait until he knew Freidman was home.

He'd changed into a pair of casual trousers and was pulling on a cotton sweater when the doorbell rang. Wondering who could be looking for him at this time, he hurried to the intercom. Honor identified herself and he buzzed her up.

Opening the door, he watched her ascend to the third floor with appreciation. She looked radiant in a peach knit outfit that set her copper hair ablaze. Only the shadowing in her eyes was a dead giveaway to her continuing inner turmoil.

"Come on in." He moved back to let her pass. "I wasn't expecting you. I left a message on your machine."

"I know. That's why I'm here. Partly why, anyway," she qualified, stopping a few feet inside the apartment and facing him squarely. "I want to help you follow up this mysterious lead."

Protective instincts rising, Dakota frowned at the suggestion. "Your coming along isn't necessary."

"For me, it is."

He didn't want to argue with her. And how could he? If Nora were his daughter, nothing would stop him from going along with her.

"I'm not following up anything at the moment." At her immediate stricken look, he explained, "The man I want to question isn't home yet."

"A man. Who?"

"Let's sit down, have a cup of coffee or something."

Though she followed him into the living room, she didn't allow herself to be distracted. "Why do I get the feeling whatever you have to say isn't going to be anything I want to hear?"

Because it was true. How was he going to tell her Seattle's most infamous racketeer might be involved in her daughter's kidnapping. "Coffee first, then I'll tell you everything I know."

Dakota sensed that didn't make her happy, but she acquiesced and sat on one of the sofas. The minicoffee maker was already set up with water and grounds at the end of the breakfast bar. All he had to do was flick a switch and he'd have four cups worth in minutes. While the coffee was brewing, he loaded a tray with mugs, napkins and spoons.

"Cream or sugar?" he asked.

"Black will be fine. I think I'm going to need the extra jolt of pure caffeine."

She was glaring at him accusingly, but all he could think of was how much he wanted to take her in his arms and kiss her.

He set the tray on the coffee table and went back for the pot. Now was not the time to get distracted, though he wouldn't take much convincing. Sitting next to Honor on the couch, he filled both mugs.

He'd barely set the pot on the tray when she snapped, "All right, let's have it."

Dakota took a sip of coffee and kept his voice casual. "I saw Lester Freidman going into the NCSC building today."

"Who?" She appeared appropriately puzzled.

"He's an accountant...and King Crawley's right-hand man."

"Crawley?" Honor's eyes grew round. "Isn't that the man your father put away?"

"You got it."

"Why would he be involved?"

"I really don't know. But he's behind a dummy company called Kingfish Entitlements that makes large contributions to NCSC."

She fell back against the couch, her face unnaturally pale. "My God, if a man as powerful as Crawley is behind Nora's kidnapping—"

"That's still to be seen," Dakota said in an effort to reassure her. He didn't want her to panic. "I'm acting on instinct here. I may be way off base, but I want to pay a visit to Lester Freidman and see if I can't cement a connection."

"I'm coming with you." She said the words so quickly, they came out almost as one.

Dakota tried to be diplomatic. "That wouldn't be wise." What he meant was he didn't think she could take the strain of coming face-to-face with such a dangerous man and still think clearly.

"I don't care. Nora is *my* daughter."

"I have just as much invested in this situation as you do." Immediately realizing the idiocy of that statement, he said, "Let me rephrase myself. I not only would like to salvage my career, but I want you to get your daughter back almost as much as you do."

Her jaw was set and her words were clipped. "I'm going, even if I have to tail you."

He should have known he couldn't win. "Then you'll wait in the car," he insisted.

"I'll wait in the car," she echoed with equal determination.

Taking another sip of the coffee, Dakota chose not to further the argument. For the time being, either of them going was a moot point since Freidman wasn't home.

"So what are you going to ask him?" Honor wanted to know. Her color was coming back, two bright spots against her translucent skin. "How are you going to get at the truth?"

Considering he hadn't yet figured that out—he was pretty good at thinking on his feet and had surmised he'd play it by ear—he evaded her questions. "We'll talk about it later. In the meantime, why don't we get something to eat."

Honor agreed, but from her expression, he could tell he wouldn't change her mind. He should have known better than to tantalize her with the information and then expect her to sit and wait it out.

Honor Bright was as stubborn and as focused as they came—two more reasons to love her.

HONOR LIKED THE CASUAL seafood restaurants on the pier. After buying fried oysters and shrimp, salads and chips, and large containers of beer from a take-out window, they sat in the open at a rough-hewn wood table with bench seats. The view of Puget Sound was spectacular. This was Seattle at its most beautiful: a clear evening, blue sky, setting sun spilling its brilliant rays across the water.

A backdrop for romance.

Honor only wished she were up to the promise with Dakota at her side. At the moment, her mind was going round and round with thwarted anticipation . . . as was her stomach.

"You're frowning," he commented. "Something wrong with the oysters?"

"They're wonderful."

"You haven't touched them."

"I've eaten here before."

Dakota chewed and swallowed a whole shrimp in seconds. "Feel like talking?"

"About what? How anxious I am? How much I fear I'll never see my daughter again?"

"I was hoping for something more positive," he said, continuing to eat voraciously. "Tell me about Nora."

"Come on, you don't want to hear all that baloney that parents think to themselves—like she's the neatest kid ever to walk the earth."

He chuckled and stopped with a chip halfway to his mouth. "What makes her so neat?"

"I don't know. Certainly not her clothes," she said with a smile, playing on the meaning. "She's always into something, getting herself mussed and dirty. Then she has to change—sometimes four or five times a day."

"And this is voluntary?"

Honor nodded and took a bite of oyster, which really was delicious. "She's only four, but she seems so grown-up, and has definite opinions on things."

"Like?"

"Like not wanting to move from place to place. She told me the stress wasn't good for *my* complexion." Honor smiled at the memory. Thinking about it made her feel closer to Nora. "And she said that going on location all the time made me lonely."

"Were you?"

"Sometimes, but it's difficult to be too lonely with a child around."

"Maybe she was conveying her own insecurities," Dakota suggested. "So you never left her with a nanny?"

"Of course not. She was my daughter. *Is* my daughter. I would never be without her if I could help it."

"Is she much like you—a hoyden?"

Honor laughed. She'd forgotten she'd admitted that to him. "I'm afraid so. She's always running helter-skelter, getting into everything. And she's already developed a strong personality. I remember one time going to pick her up from her play group a bit early. She had several little boys running around, fetching things for her."

"Sounds like they were infatuated. Knowing her mother, I can understand that."

An electric moment passed between them and Honor realized how much she'd grown to depend on this man. Dakota knew just what to do, just what to say to reassure her and strengthen her resolve. Even getting her to talk about Nora had been a positive stroke. She was feeling closer to the child who was her heart than she had since they'd been separated.

By getting her to talk about Nora, Dakota had made the relationship more tangible for her again when somehow she had oddly distanced herself from her daughter. She'd been reluctant to think or talk about Nora lest she be unable to go on. But she hadn't reacted that way at all. Rather, she felt as if Nora were there with them. At the very least, her hope was renewed.

Honor knew she really *could* count on Dakota in her daughter's case.

And in her own . . . well, the intense way he was looking at her . . .

Oddly flustered, she concentrated on her food, her appetite suddenly voracious. Finished with his own dinner, Dakota excused himself to call Freidman. He returned a few minutes later, his expression one of disappointment.

"He's still not home."

"Maybe we should park outside his house until he returns."

"We may be in for a long wait."

"Do you have a better plan?"

They left for Freidman's place less than a half hour later. On their way to the Magnolia area not far from downtown, Honor thought about what they might find if they searched the empty house. Dakota presented a problem there, however. She doubted she could get him to break in. He had an immovable set of ethics, while she—in order to get her daughter back—was willing to do whatever it took.

She was somewhat disappointed when they arrived at the waterfront area on a high bank overlooking Puget Sound. The Tudor-style home Dakota identified as belonging to the accountant was brightly lit against the night sky.

"He's here, after all," Dakota said.

Honor's heart hammered in a combination of excitement and dread. Maybe now they would learn something that would lead them to Nora. She only hoped they weren't putting her daughter in even more danger, though it was a little late for that kind of speculation.

Dakota parked the car and released his seat belt. When she did the same, he said, "You're staying in the car, remember?"

"But—"

"No *buts*."

Honor clenched her jaw. She'd stay in the car, all right, until he got in the house—assuming he could talk his way in. Then she would do what she pleased. That she didn't argue, merely sat there passively staring at him, seemed to convince Dakota she would do as he told her.

"Relax," he said softly. "I can handle this. Make yourself inconspicuous so he doesn't see you."

With that order, he left the car and strode purposefully toward the house.

Tension roiled through Honor as she watched him climb the wide steps and wait for Freidman to answer the bell. The man who came to the door was as thin as what was left of his graying black hair. Slinking low in her seat, she rolled down her window and strained to hear the conversation, picking up enough bits and pieces to follow along.

"... Want to talk to you ... Kingfish Entitlements," Dakota was saying.

"You can ... office hours."

"I'd ... this informally ... illegal ..."

"You're mistaken!" Freidman said loudly enough for Honor to hear perfectly. "Kingfish Entitlements is being run in a perfectly legitimate manner."

"Then you won't mind talking about it."

Honor could tell Freidman wasn't thrilled, but he moved from the doorway. With a last glance toward the car—undoubtedly to make sure she stayed put—Dakota entered the house.

The door was barely closed behind him before Honor was out of the vehicle. She forced herself to wait for a moment, to give them time to become so absorbed in what was sure to be an argument that neither man would see her. Then she set off, cursing the peach knit that seemed to glow in the moonlight and the high heels that made it difficult to travel fast.

She did the best she could, all the while keeping her eyes on the living room windows. Freidman sat with his back to her, Dakota facing her. She'd almost made it by them both when Dakota—as if instinct warned him—looked her way. That he saw her registered in his features for a split second, but he immediately covered, turning his full attention back to the man he was questioning.

Dakota was trying to assure her safety.

Sticking close to the red-brick house, which was separated from its nearest neighbor by a dozen yards or so, Honor realized she would hear about her foolishness the moment Dakota was done with Freidman. She didn't look forward to the quarrel that was sure to ensue.

She rounded the building and stopped at the edge of the spacious backyard lined by a veritable forest of conifers and deciduous trees. Not knowing what she might find, she searched for some evidence of a child's presence. Not a single toy lay within her line of vision. Quietly, she tiptoed up the back steps leading to the kitchen until a creaking board froze her to the spot.

The distinct sensation of being watched crawled through her. She spun around. Giant sentinels, the moonlit trees alone cast their menacing shadows across the lawn.

Good Lord, she had to stop being so jumpy!

Palms sweating, she continued her ascent, skirting the windows until she was certain no noise came from within. Then she inched toward one of the glass panes. Her gaze swept the neat kitchen and the doorway leading to the living room. All she spied were long legs she identified as belonging to Dakota. No sign of a child.

Stairs zigzagged overhead. Dare she follow them to the second floor?

How could she not?

Hoping not to make any more noise than necessary, she slipped out of her heels and, carrying them, sneaked up the steps, all the while trying to shake the intense sensation of being watched. Her breathing kept time with the rush of her pulse. Wanting to believe she was imagining things didn't stop her from looking around when she got to the second-floor landing.

Seeing no one, she took a gulp of air and turned to the door that led into a hallway. The handle didn't turn. Locked! Damn!

The window to the left was softly illuminated. She peered inside. A bedroom. Neat without frills. A necktie on the chest. Probably Freidman's.

Glancing over her shoulder as she did so, Honor moved back past the door to the window on the other side, this one dark. Her gaze swept the moonlit interior over the hulking shadows made by furniture. Even in the dark, the room seemed sterile and unlived in.

A loud metallic noise from behind startled Honor. She turned and inspected the large area beyond the house. Three buildings stood among the greenery—a semi-open gazebo, a small tool shed and a long, brick, multicar garage. No movement identified any human presence.

Descending the stairs, she checked the kitchen window. Dakota was still in place. She couldn't give up yet.

At the sidewalk, she slipped into her heels, hesitating only a short moment before proceeding to check out the three other buildings.

Nothing in the gazebo.

The tool shed was locked.

The garage was dark.

But something kept her from rushing back to the street. Nothing tangible, merely instinct. That noise had been caused by something.

Rather, *someone.*

She circled the garage, the lawn's moisture soaking the expensive leather of her shoes. A tall hedge lined the back of the property, but through the gaps between branches, she saw an odd shape. An object, dark and hulking.

Her step quickened.

Could that be a car? But why in back of the garage rather than inside? Why, if not to hide if from the casual observer?

She was at the bushes, her hand snaking an opening through the branches when she heard yet another noise. A loud crunch. A footfall?

Nervously peering behind her, she was relieved when she saw nothing.

Still her hand trembled as it parted the bushes.

Another crunch, closer this time. A small animal, she told herself. Intent on seeing the car parked behind the garage, she hugged the bushes and widened the gap between branches. She had a clear view of the trunk area of a dark Plymouth and its vanity license plate.

HOTSHOT jumped out at her as did the sound of movement from behind.

Now certain she wasn't alone, Honor spun around to see who was sneaking up behind her!

Chapter Ten

Before Honor got so much as a glimpse of her attacker, a hand clamped firmly over her mouth and an arm snaked across her chest. She fought like a wild woman and tried to bite the hand so she could free her mouth and scream.

"Cut it out!" Dakota whispered heatedly, tightening his grip on her shoulders and dragging her back toward the house. "Let's get out of here before Freidman realizes I didn't go straight to the car."

Though she stopped struggling and he let her go but for a grip on her wrist, Honor was furious. How dare Dakota frighten her like that! She felt as if the Indy 500 were being run through her vascular track. Her legs pumped like mad to keep up with Dakota, who was jogging if not actually running by the house.

As they passed the living room windows, she saw Freidman on the telephone. His back to them, the accountant was having a serious conversation with someone.

Her heartbeat didn't steady until they were in the car and crawling away from the curb. They'd driven past several other stately homes before Dakota finally turned on the car lights and accelerated.

"How could you do that to me?" Honor demanded.

"Do that?" he repeated vehemently. "I saved your fanny, lady. You were supposed to stay put in the car."

"I don't take orders well."

"No kidding. Heaven help your film directors! What the hell were you up to?"

"Looking around," she said tersely, irritated by the reference to her work.

"To find what?"

"Some sign that my daughter had been there."

"A man like Freidman wouldn't be stupid enough to bring a kidnapped child to his own home. I could have predicted you wouldn't learn anything."

Though she was already cooling off, Honor couldn't help challenging him after what she *had* found. "And I suppose Freidman was a font of information, eager to spill his guts to you."

"Not exactly. He wouldn't admit to anything, so all I succeeded in doing was warning him." Dakota's ire faded, to be replaced with self-disgust. "But at least I made him nervous. I'm pretty sure he knows a lot more than he's saying."

"I'm positive he does."

"You *did* find something?" he asked, turning the car toward the downtown area.

"Just before you gave me the fright of my life. A car was parked behind the garage—a dark Plymouth with a license plate that reads HOTSHOT."

"HOT..." His voice faded off in amazement. "That must be the car that followed me!"

"You never told me you saw the license plate."

"How should I know it would be important? Besides, I only saw the HOT part," Dakota added. "Wait a minute. If I didn't tell you about the license plate, then why did *you* realize it was significant?"

"Because of that first night when I went down to the docks to deliver the information," Honor said. "The area was deserted except for three other parked cars. That Plymouth was one of them."

Dakota let out a whistle. "It might not stand up as evidence in court, but it's enough to convince me Crawley is behind this deal, working through Freidman."

"So what do we do with this information?"

"I go to my father and ask for his help."

Honor didn't protest. Involving Judge Jasper Raferty was the next thing to involving the police. But Nora had been gone for more than seventy-two hours now. Adding to Honor's fear was the knowledge that the criminals were now aware of her association with Dakota. Not only had he warned Freidman, but she was certain someone had been watching her, namely, the owner of that car.

She only hoped Judge Raferty could help, because, considering they were dealing with a powerful man whose reach prison bars couldn't stop, Honor just didn't see how she and Dakota were going to resolve anything without outside assistance.

DAKOTA WAS STILL TRYING to figure out how exactly to approach his father with their problem as he ascended to the top of Queen Anne Hill and pulled up in front of the elegant brick colonial that was his family home. Not that any of the family other than Jasper Raferty himself had lived there for the past half dozen years since Asia had declared her independence. In addition to the judge, an aging butler and a middle-aged housekeeper were the mansion's only occupants.

Dakota left the car in the circular drive and thought how he'd hated having to drop off Honor, to once again leave her alone with her uncertainties and fear. He hadn't seen any other choice.

When his father found out what he'd gotten himself involved in...

Judge Jasper Raferty was an incredibly righteous man with a short fuse. He wouldn't hold back his disapproval concerning Honor's methods of obtaining the ransom. Dakota hadn't wanted to put her through the lecture on honesty and trust and the law his father would be sure to give.

The front door opened before he could get to it, the butler looking on him with surprise.

"Mr. Dakota, a pleasure to see you." Ford smiled, the elderly man's mottled face breaking into dozens of tiny wrinkles. "Judge Raferty didn't tell me you were expected."

"That's because he didn't know I was coming, Ford. Where can I find him?"

"On the terrace, going over a case. Some consulting work or other."

As if his father didn't have enough to keep him busy as a superior court judge. "At this hour?"

Ford shrugged and closed the door. "Perhaps you can talk to him, get him to ease up."

"Work is my father's life."

Dakota strode through the house that had once been filled with antiques. Claiming there was too much clutter, Jasper had taken to selling off the furniture from the unused rooms a couple of years before. Now Dakota noticed the main rooms were beginning to look barren.

He stepped from the living room onto the terrace, which overlooked formal English gardens. Below lay downtown Seattle and Puget Sound, and in the distance, the mountains. Ensconced in an oversize rattan chair, Jasper Raferty seemed impervious to all but his work as he read papers that lay atop a stack of manila folders on the table before him.

"Good evening, Father."

Looking up, the older man registered surprise. "Son, good to see you!" He slipped the papers into the top folder. "Must be important, your dropping by at this hour."

"It's important." Dakota sat on the padded wicker chair opposite his father. No use wasting time with pleasantries. He might as well get it over with. "This has to do with King Crawley."

"Crawley?" His father immediately shoved the stack of folders into a briefcase on the table. "What about him?"

"I'm certain he's had a child kidnapped and I'm helping the mother get her daughter back safely."

"What?" The older man sounded appalled. "Who is this woman and what's your involvement with her?"

Taking a deep breath, Dakota filled him in on all that had transpired, from Honor's break-in to the latest development with her identification of the Plymouth— leaving out the details of his growing personal involvement. Certain his father would explode with indignation, he was surprised when the judge sat very still and quiet, as though he were in shock. His skin appeared to have grown pasty, and his large-knuckled fingers clenched and unclenched the arms of the chair.

"What do *you* think Crawley had to gain?" the older man finally asked.

Dakota had the oddest feeling that his father had his own opinion and wanted to compare it with his son's.

"Obviously, he has a strong interest in the salmon-fishing industry or he wouldn't be involved with NCSC. For a while, I had thought this whole thing might be personal against me," Dakota admitted. "Now, I'm not so sure. Maybe Crawley agreed to get rid of any hostile eyewitnesses against the companies doing the illegal fishing."

"Maybe." The judge didn't sound at all convinced.

"We know he isn't above murder."

The Judge said nothing.

Dakota shifted uneasily. It wasn't like his father to be reflective when one of his children was in trouble. Normally, Jasper Raferty would rant and rave and lead the charge to the rescue as he had when Sydney's supposed husband had died mere weeks before. Family was all-important to him. But now, he was acting against type.

"Father, what aren't you telling me?"

"Can't an old man have a few private thoughts?" Jasper blustered, rising quickly. He indicated Dakota should do the same. "You go on home now and get some sleep. Mr. King Crawley and I are going to have a little chat tomorrow, as soon as I can clear my court schedule. I'll let you know if I find out anything that will help."

Dakota wasn't exactly satisfied with the answer, but he sensed he wouldn't get more out of his father at this time. He was going to have to be patient, but he didn't think he would rest easy until he got some definitive answers.

"All right, I'll talk to you tomorrow, then."

Leaving, Dakota had the oddest feeling. Surely his father, tyrant of the superior court, couldn't be afraid. . . .

HONOR DIDN'T KNOW HOW long she sat on the front porch swing before a chill chased her inside. As had been the case for the past few days, she'd been avoiding the too-quiet rooms.

Wandering around the living room, she couldn't avoid the pictures of Nora on the mantel. She remembered Dakota making her talk about Nora, how much closer she'd felt to her daughter by doing so. Quickly changing into a knee-length sleepshirt decorated with palm trees, she grabbed Nora's favorite quilt and brought it downstairs, where she spread it out in front of the fireplace.

The night was cool enough for a small fire. No sooner had she touched a match to the logs and picked up the framed portrait of the two of them than she heard a car pull up outside. Pressing the photograph to her pounding heart, she raced to the windows.

Dakota had returned.

She opened the door and waited for his long-legged stride to bring him to the porch. Since he hadn't said anything about seeing her again that night, something important must have brought him back. Her fingers curled around the frame of the portrait so hard, they hurt.

"What is it?" she asked anxiously. "Did your father know something helpful?"

He shook his head. "But he's going to see Crawley tomorrow and get the truth out of him if he can. I came back because I wanted to make sure you were all right. And because I wanted to be with you."

Disappointment warred with gratitude and something else—something more personal. He was gazing at her steadily and the expression in his eyes thrilled her. Honor knew she wanted to be with Dakota, as well.

"Come in. I just lit a fire. We can have a brandy, if you like."

Dakota tended to the drinks while Honor set the photo on the quilt and gathered pillows from the couches. She was on her knees arranging them in a comfortable pile when he kicked off his shoes and sat down next to her.

"Rainbows and clouds?" His eyebrows raised as he studied the pattern beneath them. "I wouldn't have guessed it to be your style."

"It's Nora's." She took her drink and touched the glass to his before taking a sip. The brandy fired its way down to her bare toes. "I remembered how much better I felt after talking about Nora. I thought I would feel close to her by thinking about some of the good times we've had together."

A lock of ash-blond hair brushing his forehead, Dakota sipped at his brandy and set the glass behind him before relaxing against the pillows.

"That's good," he said. "We're going to get her back, you know."

Eyes suddenly filling, Honor nodded and took another sip. "It's just . . . sometimes . . ."

He took her glass and set it next to his, then pulled her into the shelter of his arms and forced her head onto one of the broad shoulders she'd come to depend on during the past few days. He didn't say anything, merely stroked her hair. Her fingers curled into his sweater, a more intense shade of blue-green than his eyes.

Honor sighed and snuggled in closer, satisfied when he tightened his hold on her. She was feeling so relaxed, she was having a difficult time keeping her eyes open. But she didn't want to fall asleep just yet. She wanted to talk about Nora. Maybe she would have good dreams, then, instead of the nightmares she so feared.

"I bought this nightshirt in Maui," she said. "Nora has one just like it."

"You were on location in Hawaii?"

"Vacation—last year. Just a few days, but it was wonderful. Nora loves the water. She knew how to swim practically before she learned to walk, so we took a snorkeling lesson. There's a picture of her in her gear on the mantle," Honor said, pointing.

Dutifully, Dakota loosened his grip and sat up enough to see. "You mean the funny-looking little water sprite in the big mask?"

Honor smiled. "Nora couldn't get enough of looking at those tropical fish through that mask, let me tell you. She wore me out."

"Kids. They have resources of energy adults don't even know about. I've always wondered what it would be like to have some of my own."

"What? Energy?"

"No, children." He raised his eyebrows at her. "As if you didn't get my drift."

Thinking he'd make a terrific father, Honor asked, "Don't you like to be teased?"

"Depends on who's doing the teasing."

He was teasing her now by running a finger down the side of her cheek. And then he was doing the same to her lips by nipping at them and withdrawing.

Honor soon had enough of that. She wrapped a hand around Dakota's neck and pulled his head closer. Slanting her lips, she nudged at his until they opened and accepted hers. And then all lighthearted pretense swept away under his powerful onslaught. He kissed her until she was breathless, until she came alive under the hands that cradled her back and her hip. Heat seared her through the thin material.

As quickly as he'd fanned the flames, he doused them. He ended the kiss and lay back against the pillows, pulling her with him so her head rested against his chest. She could hear his heart beat furiously through the cotton sweater, but he was refusing to act on the passion they'd stirred in each other.

He was refusing to take advantage of her at a time when he thought she wasn't thinking straight, Honor realized.

"Close your eyes," he whispered, stroking her hair. "Relax. Sleep."

The flames in the fireplace danced before her tired eyes. She'd been afraid to close them since Nora had been kidnapped. But now, with Dakota holding her like this . . .

Her eyelids drooped and her lashes brushed her cheeks.

That he was there for her when he didn't need to be filled her with wonder. She'd never been able to count on any man before. Not the father she'd never known. Not the husband who'd never been there for her.

But Dakota, this virtual stranger who owed her nothing, wanted nothing from her, gave her everything that was important to her. If she didn't stop herself, Honor realized, she was going to find herself madly, hopelessly in love with the man.

KING CRAWLEY HAD BEEN waiting for this day for nearly three years. It was worth the wait to see Judge Jasper Raferty stand there, for once without the upper hand.

"Do you always pay social calls to men you've incarcerated?" Crawley asked insolently.

"You know why I'm here."

"Sit. Take a load off. Wanna cup of coffee?" Without waiting for an answer, Crawley signaled the guard. "Two coffees here. Cream or sugar, Raferty?"

The guard looked to the judge, who indicated he should leave. And Crawley knew why. He sat back and savored the result of his handiwork. As Raferty took a seat on the opposite side of the table, the man looked older, more worn. He'd look even worse before Crawley was through.

"What is your involvement in NCSC?" Raferty asked stiffly, his pale blue eyes narrowing threateningly.

"NCSC?" Crawley puckered his forehead and feigned innocence. "What's that?"

"You know damn well what I'm talking about!"

"Hey, Judge, don't get your dander up. Men your age have heart attacks, you know?"

The two men glared at each other, filling the small space with enough hatred in those seconds to last the average person a lifetime.

"What about NCSC?" Raferty asked. His hands were wrapped around a chair back. His knuckles stood out in white relief against the brown-painted wood. "Are you somehow using that organization to carry through with your threat to seek revenge against me?"

"Revenge? I'm behind bars. What kind of a threat does that make me?"

"Let's not play games here—"

"Let's not," Crawley interrupted with the assurance of a man who knew he had control of a situation. "I don't have time for games no more. And I don't have the patience. Not after what's happened to my family since you sentenced me to rot in this hellhole."

"Your actions sentenced you to prison."

"But you could have changed that—you agreed to. You should have stuck to your bargain, Raferty. Then you wouldn't have this guilty conscience that makes you imagine things." Crawley waited merely a beat before adding, "Olive couldn't stand the guilt after what went down at my trial."

He thought of the innocent, lovely woman who'd never had anything to do with the business. She was always a little fragile, but she was the sweetest wife and the most loving mother a man could hope for.

"She snapped—tried to commit suicide—did you know that?" Crawley could tell Raferty didn't. "What would you care what happens to another man's family once you're through with him? My own wife doesn't even remember me. From what I've been told, Olive spends her days and nights wandering around that big mansion talking to herself."

"So get her help. You've got the money to—"

"But *I'm* stuck in prison, remember? Where you put me."

Raferty ignored that. "You have children who can take care of her."

Crawley laughed. "My daughter disappeared a couple of months after you passed sentence—after being raped by one of my enemies. I couldn't protect her in here. The man wouldn't let her alone. Now I don't even know if she's alive."

The judge's pallor looked grayer than it had when he'd come through the door, if that were possible.

"Your son—"

"Hates my guts," Crawley said. "Dominic never was part of the business. He steered clear of anything I had my hands in. He was building himself quite a career. Might have made it to CEO of some fancy corporation. But the verdict and your sentence ended that dream for him. Ended his marriage, too."

"None of that's my fault."

Crawley glared at Raferty but kept his voice deceptively calm. "A man wants to protect his family. His wife. His children. But sometimes it's impossible...."

He knew Raferty got the picture when the man said, "You're trying to ruin him, aren't you?"

"Ruin who?"

"My son. You're trying to ruin Dakota because of me."

"I never said that."

"I thought you weren't going to play games. If you want revenge," Raferty pleaded, "you take it out on me, not on my family."

Crawley finally gave up the pretense. "An eye for an eye, Judge. That's from the Bible. Didn't know I read it, did you? I been reading the Bible a lot lately. I gotta be ready when I meet my maker."

"Take your revenge out on me, damn you!" Raferty demanded.

"That's what I plan on doing." Crawley leaned forward, took particular delight in spelling it out for him. "Your kid will hate you as much as Dominic hates me when I'm done with him. He won't be able to look at you without remembering that you made a deal with the devil."

"But I didn't go through with it!"

"Think that'll make any difference to an upright citizen who works in the public interest? Especially after his life is ruined like Dominic's was?"

"I'll see you pay for this, Crawley!"

"I'm already paying, Raferty. And there's nothing more you can do to me even if you could prove anything, which you can't. I'm already in this stinking hole...and I'm dying, to boot." He savored the judge's startled expression. "Didn't know that, either, did you? It's true. Liver cancer. I got maybe a year. I started making my plans the day I got *that* sentence. So what do I care about what you can do to me?"

Already looking defeated, Raferty turned and moved to the door.

Crawley laughed and called after him, "But before I die, I'll see your son can't get any work but at some menial job. He'll hate you for that, Raferty. He'll curse you every day for the rest of his life!"

Crawley's laughter died with the closing door. He'd have his revenge if it was the last thing he ever did . . . which it might very well be.

Chapter Eleven

Honor waited until she heard Gail leave her desk to make her move. She peered out of her office and saw the receptionist pull the door to the executive suite closed behind her.

She was alone in the area. Zahniser and the others and their secretaries had all gone to lunch...as had Andrew Vaughn.

And she was getting to be an expert at breaking into peoples' offices. Only this time, breaking in wasn't necessary. Vaughn hadn't bothered to lock his door behind him. Probably no one did during the day unless they were hiding something. The thought deflated her, made her think that perhaps she was wasting her time.

Honor entered the lobbyist's messy office anyway, wondering exactly how much time she had. It could take years to plow through the stacks of papers and files littering every horizontal surface. She started with the filing cabinets, intending to look for anything that had to do with contributions to NCSC in general and, more specifically, with Kingfish Entitlements.

As she began with the top drawer, Honor's thoughts strayed to Dakota—the way she'd fallen asleep in his arms, the way he'd kissed her awake early this morning, the way they'd made breakfast together. There was something so natural about the picture, though it was missing a single element, namely a little girl with copper braids. She was certain Nora would be caught by Dakota's charm just as she had been.

Back to the task at hand.

The files were as much a mess as the rest of the office, often not hung even close to the right letter. She had to stay herself from alphabetizing as she plowed ahead. Instead, she checked everything twice.

Sometime later, Honor admitted Vaughn's files contained nothing of consequence. Trying to connect the lobbyist with the kidnapping had been a wild card, one she hadn't thought of until that very morning. The hours had dragged until she'd been able to start her search, and now it seemed all for nothing. Either the man wasn't involved, or he was too smart to keep any evidence where it could be found by some amateur detective like herself!

Wanting to leave, she eyed Vaughn's desk. The several-inch-high catastrophe made her shudder. How in the world could the man find anything? She might as well go through the materials as long as she was there. She didn't even have to be careful about putting things back carefully. Vaughn wouldn't be likely to notice anything out of place.

A copy of the *Northwest Eye* sat on top. The picture of a crying raggedy child accompanied by a story written by Karen Lopinski got to her. She set the tabloid aside to reveal correspondence, brochures, memos and unopened mail in a jumble. Honor gave each piece a cursory glance as she dug down layer by layer. Halfway through the pile, she knocked into a stack that went sliding off the desk, papers flying in every direction.

"Damn!"

Stooping, she gathered a handful of envelopes and papers that she dropped on top of the heap. Then she had to get on her hands and knees to reach others which had slid under the desk and computer table. She barely glanced at them until she found a memo from Zahniser. Stopping for a second, she skimmed the contents. Her eyes widened and she sat back on her heels to reread the short missive.

We cannot continue to operate with a lobbyist who draws the ire of those companies we are paid to work for. Therefore, your services will no longer be needed by NCSC as of August 31.

Have your desk and office cleared of any personal effects on or before that date so your replacement can get to work as soon as possible.

Vaughn, fired?

No one had said anything about the lobbyist leaving. He'd even sat in on the meeting with Dakota, though Dakota had admitted the other man had been oddly quiet. Then she remembered the Monday morning meeting she'd attended and the argument Vaughn had had with Zahniser after dragging him out into the hallway. She checked the date of the memo. Monday. This must have been what they were arguing about! Had Vaughn found a way to change Zahniser's mind since?

Blackmail, perhaps?

That would explain why he was acting as if he were conducting business as usual.

"Find what you were looking for?"

Honor started and met Vaughn's eyes. Wreathed in cigar smoke, he stood in the doorway, his glower making her pulse rush.

"Goodness, you startled me!" she said, hoping she sounded as innocent as she was trying to act.

Eyes narrowing, he asked, "Have some reason to feel guilty?"

Her mind quickly raced for an explanation as she slipped the memo to the bottom of the stack of papers in her hand and rose to her feet.

"I, uh, needed one of those new brochures on Coho Industries," she said, then added lamely, "I have a meeting there next week about an appearance. Everyone was out to lunch, and I figured if anyone had an extra brochure, it would be you. I didn't think you would mind if I looked for it." She indicated the papers she was holding. "I got a little clumsy." She even made a cute little grimace. "Sorry."

All through her hurried speech, Vaughn stared at her, his expression suspicious. He continued to regard her silently as he took the stack of papers from her hand and dumped them on top of the desk. Then, amazingly, he went directly to a pile on the right side and pulled out the Coho Industries brochure as if he knew exactly where everything was, and held it out.

"You do have one," she said, keeping up the pretense as she took it from him. That he wasn't saying anything was making her even more nervous. "Great. Thanks."

She felt his eyes bore into her back as she darted out of his office and into her own. Once inside, she closed the door and leaned against it until her pulse steadied

Then she went to her desk and made a pretense of looking over the brochure—in case Vaughn trailed her there—all the while concentrating on the information in the memo.

She'd just proved that Vaughn and Zahniser couldn't possibly be working together. One or the other, she thought. Could Zahniser be the guilty one with Vaughn blackmailing him so he could keep his job? Or could the lobbyist have an agenda all his own and so hadn't cared how much he'd annoyed Zahniser because he felt he had the upper hand?

Gradually, the surrounding offices came back to life. Honor heard people enter and cross through the reception area. Telephones rang. Conversations were exchanged. Having stalled as long as she cared to, Honor took her purse from her desk drawer and left her office.

"You coming back this afternoon?" Gail asked.

"Nope, nothing planned," Honor told the receptionist.

That was true. She was playing it by ear, waiting for Dakota's father to confront King Crawley. Of course, she had no idea of what that would prove. Crawley would undoubtedly deny any connection to the kidnapping and she would have no more idea of how to find her daughter than she'd had the night before. She didn't think Crawley's type intimidated easily, not even when faced with the wrath of a judge.

She kept trying to find something more positive to think about as she drove toward her Capitol Hill home. But by the time she'd parked her car in the drive and climbed her front steps, she was in a worse mood than before. Speculation bred more speculation. No proof of anything. And when she entered the house and the phone recorder yielded no call from the kidnappers, she sank into a deep depression.

Standing over the machine, continuing to stare at the steady red light, she felt a chill go through her. She rubbed the gooseflesh from her arms and looked around the room. Something about the house didn't feel quite right . . . but, of course, it wouldn't, she told herself.

Nora's absence was affecting her every waking moment, whether or not she was constantly aware of that fact, Honor thought.

And how could it not?

Her mind spinning, she paced the living room that, rather than being comfortable in its familiarity, felt cold and foreign and filled with threatening shadows. The very atmosphere made her recount the nightmare: Four days since her daughter was snatched from the Space Needle. Two days since she'd delivered the last set of papers. A dangerous racketeer involved in the kidnapping plot. Still no clues about her daughter's whereabouts.

Assuming Nora was still alive.

What if the reason she hadn't heard was because the kidnappers realized they didn't have the information they wanted? What if they'd grown tired of taking care of and pacifying a four-year-old? If only Dakota could have put her daughter's welfare above his own professional reputation.

Even as she thought it, Honor knew she wasn't playing fair. Dakota was working both sides of the street, protecting more than one life. He'd told her so when he'd let her see the contents of the folder. And King

Crawley's involvement only confirmed that fact. The man was a murderer—rather, he had his henchman do his dirty work for him. His reach went beyond steel bars.

What if Nora...

A chill shot through Honor as though she really weren't alone...as though the house held another presence...as though Nora were here with her in spirit if not in...

She couldn't finish the thought, wouldn't consider the worst, or she would have no reason to go on. She was nearly ready to go out of her mind as it was. The impossibility of her situation was beginning to seem magnified by leaps and bounds. And everything that had happened since Sunday was all her fault. From the first, she'd made one mistake after another, starting with trying to get Nora back on her own rather than calling the police.

Well, she couldn't get Nora back, and neither could Dakota, but maybe the police could, she finally admitted. They were trained for this sort of thing. She would have to call them. Listening to people who kidnapped little girls had been the biggest mistake she'd ever made. She'd deluded herself into believing the authorities couldn't do what she had to. She couldn't gamble with her daughter's life any longer.

She was going to call the police *now,* before she changed her mind!

Determined to carry through immediately, she crossed to the telephone, unable to shake off the uneasy feeling that followed her. She found herself looking over her shoulder, staring at innocent shadows.

Closing her eyes and taking a deep breath for courage, she reached for the telephone. Her fingers trembled as they curled around the plastic. Before she could pick up the receiver, however, she sensed a real presence behind her. Before she could turn, an arm quickly snaked around her throat.

"Don't turn around."

The whispered command was familiar, the same voice she'd heard at the Space Needle.

For a moment, Honor froze even as her pulse kicked into overdrive. "My daughter—you've brought her back to me?"

"You've been pressing your luck—"

"What about Nora?" Honor cried, trying to turn in the kidnapper's arms despite his greater strength.

Her head was snapped in response and the pressure on her throat increased in silent, painful warning. She stopped struggling instantly.

"You want to see the kid alive?" came the whisper. "Then don't do anything foolish. Stop playing cops and robbers. You've been tempting fate with your amateur-detective bull. You're just no good at it, so cut it out and follow orders. You have one more chance—*only one*—to do as you are told. Understand?"

Honor nodded. Keeping her face averted from the telephone, the man picked up the receiver and shoved it into her hand. Then he dialed a number she couldn't see.

"Use it," he whispered.

He let up on the pressure and she put the receiver to her ear. "Hello?"

"Mommy!" came Nora's squeal.

"Nora, b-baby." She couldn't help herself. Her voice broke. "You're all right, aren't you?"

"You sound funny."

Honor realized she had to pretend for Nora's sake. "Mommy's getting a cold, honey."

"Then I gotta be with you."

"You can't right now."

"But who's gonna take care of you?"

Honor bit down on the inside of her lip and swallowed hard. "I'll be okay, peaches. I'm feeling better already. Honest."

"Mommy, I miss you." Her little girl voice was wistful and close to breaking. "How come I can't come on location this time? You always brought me before."

"This time is special." She hoped to God Nora never realized how special. "It won't be much longer, I promise. You be a good girl and do everything they tell you."

"They? You mean Mrs. Murphy?"

"That's right," Honor said.

Mrs. Murphy—maybe knowing the name could help somehow. Or so she thought before remembering the warning about playing detective. Obviously *they* knew her every move. When the man behind her gave her a sharp nudge in the kidneys, she knew she had to wind up the conversation.

"I'm going to have to go now."

"But I don't wanna stay here no more," Nora protested, suddenly breaking into sobs that tore at Honor's heart. "The other kids are okay, but I wanna be with *you*."

Chest squeezing tight, Honor forced herself to speak calmly. "I wish I could be with you, too, peaches."

"I wanna go home," her daughter cried shrilly, an unheard of hysteria creeping into her voice.

"Nora, take it easy."

"No!" she screamed. "I won't."

The line went dead.

"Nora!" Honor cried. "Nora! Talk to me."

But only a dial tone answered.

And Honor realized she was alone. The pressure had been removed from her neck. She whipped around. The man was gone. Panic welled in her breast as she realized she didn't have the first inkling of what she was supposed to do next.

Hang up the telephone, a little voice inside whispered. *Maybe they'll call back and tell you.*

But as she hung up the receiver, she noticed something bright and familiar lying next to the base. Honor dropped the telephone and a scream of agony caught in her throat.

Her heart pounded so hard she thought it would burst through the wall of her chest. The ensuing sobs that escaped her matched that intensity and she felt a pain more physical than any she'd experienced. Tears flooded her eyes and soaked her cheeks and neck as she reached out to pick up the warning left by the kidnapper.

Pressing the silky reminder of her daughter to her chest, Honor cried as if her heart would break. She couldn't stop if her life depended on it. If she didn't do exactly as they said, they would kill her baby. She saw that as clearly as she had ever understood anything.

Wailing, she slid down the wall and rolled herself up into a ball, fist pressed to her chest, one of Nora's copper braids crushed in numb fingers.

"HE AS MUCH AS ADMITTED his guilt and laughed about it," Jasper Raferty told his son.

Dakota frowned as he looked at his father. Normally, the judge stood tall and straight, his carriage that of a far younger man. But now, as Jasper paced the parlor that had once been his wife's special place, Dakota noticed his father was showing his age. His face looked haggard, even older than his sixty-eight years.

Dakota didn't understand.

"What's going on, Father? You're taking this personally. Does this move to destroy my lobbying campaign have something to do with you? With the sentence you passed on Crawley?" Dakota asked, growing more uneasy by the second. As the judge continued pacing, Dakota found he couldn't control the nerves that were tying his stomach into a knot.

Jasper nodded. "This has more to do with me than I ever wanted you to know." He wiped his hand across his face and slumped down into an armchair. "I can do nothing to stop it, son. God knows I would if I could. I'm sorry."

Dakota didn't like the sound of his father's admission, but he was still trying to deny his gut feeling. "Stop what?" he asked.

"Crawley's revenge. He's taking out his hatred for me on you. He's determined to ruin you to make me suffer."

"Because you passed sentence on him, right?"

"Because I didn't carry through with my side of the bargain."

"What bargain?"

"A bargain I made with the devil." Jasper's words came out a whisper, raw and pain filled. "A bargain I knew you would hate me for. A bargain I hated myself for. That's why, in the end, I couldn't go through with it. I'd lived my entire life for the law. I couldn't go through with it," he repeated, shaking his head.

Dakota couldn't keep the chill from his voice as he asked, "Go through with what? What kind of bargain did you make with Crawley?"

"I was going to set aside some crucial evidence in the trial." Jasper met his son's gaze. "I was going to see to it that Crawley wasn't convicted."

"You would have let scum like him go free?" Dakota didn't know how he kept his control. "Why?"

"Money. Power. Crawley offered me a substantial cash payment . . . and offered to be a silent backer if I wanted to further my political career."

Dakota couldn't believe what he was hearing. "But the Rafertys have always been wealthy—"

"Used to be wealthy." Jasper shook his head. "I was greedy. Made too many bad investments. I lost the rest on Black Monday, when the stock market crashed. The Raferty wealth is gone." He seemed to be talking to himself, trying to understand how it all had happened. "As are the servants. And the furniture."

"Mother's antiques." Dakota felt dazed, as if he were walking through a bad dream. No wonder the house had been stripped bit by bit. "You've been selling them—"

"To pay for the taxes and upkeep of this place. The salary of a civil servant only goes so far."

His stomach clutched, and Dakota feared he would be sick. He'd spent his entire life trying to emulate the one man he'd thought beyond corruption. Now it seemed Judge Jasper Raferty was no better than the criminals he put behind bars. Dakota felt as if his entire life had been a lie. Fury filled him and he strode to where his father sat. He didn't try to hide his contempt as he loomed over the man who seemed to age further before his eyes.

"How could you betray everything you ever taught me to believe in, Father! You're an officer of the court—"

"I didn't go through with it," Jasper whispered, his fingers kneading the chair's arms. "I told you I couldn't. That's why he'll have his revenge on me by ruining the son I love."

"Then it is me and not the campaign Crawley is after."

"The files are merely a means to an end," his father agreed, "a way to envelope you in more negative publicity—publicity that will once and for all damage your credibility. Crawley wants to destroy your career the same way the publicity of the trial destroyed his son, Dominic's."

"What kind of cockamamie thinking is this?"

"Crawley blames me for everything that happened to his family since he was incarcerated," Jasper said. "His son was ruined both professionally and personally. His daughter was raped, then vanished. His wife was driven to the brink of insanity. She even tried to commit suicide. He blames all of that on me, all because I wouldn't go through with the deal."

"I don't want to hear you try to whitewash yourself any more!" Dakota yelled. "You could have come to me for money. Or Asia and Sydney. We would all have pulled together to keep the family home."

Jasper seemed to sink even deeper into the chair. "I made a mistake."

"It was more than a mistake, Father. It was a violation of a sacred trust."

"But I didn't—"

"You did!"

Dakota couldn't help feeling that by his one act, his father had negated everything he'd once believed in. Everything Dakota believed in. He couldn't forgive Jasper for taking that away from him.

"Crawley said he would make me suffer, and he was correct," Jasper mumbled. "I've suffered mightily since the day I agreed to the devil's bargain."

"Obviously you haven't suffered enough," Dakota said tersely, getting no satisfaction from his father's stricken expression. "Or you wouldn't have continued to 'serve' people who trusted you. How can you continue to sit on the bench and call yourself a judge?"

"I *am* a judge."

"You're a hypocrite!"

Dakota took a step back from the man who had sired him. Mentally, he was already light-years removed.

"Son—"

"Don't call me that. My father was an honorable man. I don't know you."

As Dakota turned away, Jasper's head lolled forward and he whispered, "Crawley has won, after all."

The desperate words echoed after Dakota as he slammed out of the house that had once been a home. Now it was merely a place, a shell of what it had once been, just as was Dakota's faith in the inherent goodness of humanity.

He drove his car with reckless abandon as though, with speed, he could leave behind the unpleasant things he had learned. He was actually surprised when he found himself approaching Pioneer Square. He hadn't consciously headed for home.

Home.

Though he took pride in his loft apartment, the mansion on Queen Anne Hill had always held that title. No more. There was nothing left for him in the place where he had been part of a warm, loving family. The good memories had been tainted and he didn't think he could ever forget.

Dakota parked the car and walked the half block to his building. He was so distracted he didn't see the foreign figure curled in the corner of the vestibule until she cried out and launched herself off the floor at him, wrapping her arms around his neck.

"Hold me," Honor begged. "I need you so. Don't send me away tonight."

His arms tightened around her back and when she tilted her head, he saw she had been crying.

"Let's go upstairs," he said, gently stroking her cheek. "Tonight, we need each other."

Chapter Twelve

"Something broke inside me when I saw it," Honor said, fingering Nora's braid a short while later. She was curled in the corner of a couch—alone and aching—watching Dakota pace.

"Exactly the reaction they hoped for. They want you amenable, easy to manipulate."

His flat voice shot a chill through Honor, who didn't know of the turn of events that was making him act so strangely. He had taken her in his arms and admitted he needed her; now he had withdrawn and was stalking the apartment like some cornered wild animal. What in the world was going on?

"These people are ruthless," she said, watching him carefully. "What if—"

Dakota turned on her. "Don't even think it!" he commanded with such force, she stared.

"But if Crawley *is* involved..." Shuddering at the very thought, she stuffed the braid in her jacket pocket and set the garment away from her on the back of the couch. She was waiting for Dakota's response, waiting for him to tell her what his father had learned. While his expression was purposely blank, the tension in the room was palpable.

"Freidman is orchestrating the action from the outside," he said, walking to the window as he continued to avoid that topic. "What we have to figure out is who it is he's using—we have to identify his cohort. That person must be someone we know."

"Or more than one person. Nora mentioned a Mrs. Murphy. She could be the woman in the soup-kitchen line. And that was definitely a man who broke into my home tonight!"

Arms crossed over his broad chest, Dakota asked, "Are you sure you can't remember anything about him?"

"I didn't see him. I—I wasn't thinking clearly. I'm pretty certain it wasn't Gary, though. I can't believe he would hurt me physically."

"The bastard hurt you?" Dakota was at the couch in three great strides. "How? Where?"

She looked up at him, happy to see some emotion mobilizing his face. "I might have a bruise or two on my neck. Nothing like yours," she said, her eyes straying to the discoloration on his throat.

"They're fading."

"Not fast enough."

Again he sounded removed when he said, "I'm touched that you care."

"Of course I care!"

If she hoped for a like response, Honor was disappointed. At least for the moment, Dakota was going with his intellect rather than his emotions.

"I was thinking the outside person had to be someone who was in the NCSC building when Freidman went in," he said. "A perfect venue for a meeting that wouldn't cause suspicion. Think about it—broad daylight, a public place. What could be safer, seemingly more innocent? Zahniser, Vaughn and our friendly reporter Karen Lopinski were all there. Of course, only Vaughn smokes those obnoxious cigars like the one we found near the soup kitchen."

"True," Honor said, though she was without enthusiasm for his conclusion. Something was nagging at her, something she couldn't quite pinpoint. "Freidman could simply have been delivering another contribution."

"In person? I doubt it. He's a man who wields power, not a delivery boy." Dakota quickly shifted gears as he again began pacing, this time toward the painting hiding the wall safe. "Could Vaughn have been the man who broke into your place tonight? Think hard—how big was the guy?"

Honor wrinkled her forehead as she tried to sort impressions that had been distorted by her panic. "Tall. Definitely too tall and fit to be Zahniser," she admitted, remembering the intense pressure on her throat levered from a greater height. And there had been no soft paunch pressing against her back. "It could have been Vaughn." She shook her head. "Maybe. I'm really not certain."

"That eliminates Zahniser."

"Only from attacking me. You don't think he'd do that sort of thing himself any more than Freidman would deliver a contribution, do you? More than likely, he'd send some dock worker."

Dakota looked at her as though she'd hit on something. Before he could continue questioning her or making speculations, however, she continued.

"One thing is for certain—Zahniser and Vaughn are not working together. Zahniser sent the lobbyist a notice of termination on Monday. But Vaughn isn't turning tail and packing up. He must have something on his employer."

"This throws a whole new light on things. We could work one against the other, if only we had more information."

"I'd like more information, as well." When he looked at her questioningly, Honor asked, "Are you ever going to tell me what you learned from your father?"

Dakota went so still and white, his reaction frightened her. She knew then that he had been avoiding telling her for some very personal reason.

"He betrayed everything he ever taught me to believe in," Dakota finally said, his tone bland.

"What do you mean?"

His eyes seemed to darken to the color of a roiling sea when he said, "He made a deal with Crawley to get the crook off."

Honor frowned. "But that didn't happen. Crawley's in jail."

"Only because my father got cold feet. He thinks that the fact he didn't go through with the deal excuses him."

She could tell it didn't—not in Dakota's eyes. His torment was there to read. She rose from the couch and went to him, wrapped her arms around his waist and lay her cheek against his chest. His arms circled her, loosely, devoid of his earlier passion.

"That must have been difficult for you to hear," she said softly.

"It explained so much. Remember, I told you I thought this was something personal."

"And I thought you were being paranoid—you weren't, were you?"

His head shook, ruffling the top of her hair. "Maybe we'd be wise to go after Karen Lopinski. It's odd how she just happened to rear her nasty little head at exactly the right time. I'm sure she knows more than she's been letting on."

"But will she admit as much?"

"I don't know. But I'm sure she's involved in some way. Crawley's family was ruined by the publicity surrounding his trial and sentencing. Apparently, his whole family was affected by what happened to him. His son, Dominic, was ruined professionally."

"And so Crawley is trying to ruin *you?*" Pulling back in the loose enclosure of his arms, she looked at him. "I don't understand."

"Ever heard the saying, 'The sins of the fathers are visited on the sons'? My father reneged on a deal with the devil, and as Crawley's son suffered, so must I."

Honor cupped his cheek. "Oh, Lord, Dakota, I'm so sorry."

"You have nothing to be sorry for. You're as much a victim as I am. And you're an innocent bystander in this foul game dreamed up by two twisted old men. I'm the one who should be apologizing. I judged you for breaking into my office to steal those papers. Your 'crime' of trying to save your child was petty compared to what my father had agreed to do for Crawley. Can you ever forgive me?''

''I never held it against you.''

But she wanted to hold *him* against her. And so she did, moving closer without letting his gaze stray from hers.

Suddenly, Dakota crushed her to him. She'd been waiting for just such a renewal of this fire in him. When he kissed her, she responded with passion born of more than physical desire. She had an ache in her, a need so desperate, she wasn't certain it could ever be assuaged. But she would try... for both their sakes.

He broke the deep kiss, but she snagged his neck and kept his head tilted, his eyes on her. ''Dakota,'' she whispered, ''I more than care about you...I'm...'' She swallowed hard and finished in a rush as though the words were all one. ''I'm falling in love with you.''

''God, Honor,'' he said with a groan.

Then he swept her off her feet as though she were a lightweight rather than a tall, voluptuous woman who would fit him perfectly. He took her mouth in a savage kiss that knew no end. Blindly, he found his way to the steps and climbed them to the loft area. Once upstairs, he made his way to the bed and tumbled on to it without letting her go.

The bed swayed and swished beneath them, the sound of lapping water adding to the unusual movement.

''A water bed!'' she gasped as she pulled her mouth free. She couldn't stifle a giggle. ''You don't seem the type.''

He smiled in return. ''It just felt right in here.''

Taking a quick look around as he unsnapped her white jeans and tugged them over her hips, she realized the bedroom area had an ocean theme, starting with a dune-and-water mural painting on the wall behind the bed. Around the room were displays of driftwood and shells. A startling painting of a sunset over the wild west coast with its cliffs and seastacks hung next to the bathroom door.

Dakota threw her jeans to the floor and reached over toward what looked like a radio on the bedside table. He hit a switch. Instead of music, the low roar of surf filled the room from speakers on both sides.

"Mountains downstairs, ocean up." She undid his tie and unbuttoned his shirt as he worked on his belt and zipper. "What's in the bathroom? A pool of tropical fish?"

"A rain forest. I try to help protect the environment, remember? I don't get enough of it living in the city, so I brought it into my home."

"I love it . . . and you."

"And I love you, Honor."

He kissed her softly in punctuation, then quickly shed his clothing, throwing the garments in every direction. All the while, she stared at him and stripped off her oversize orange-gold T-shirt and matching bikinis.

When he settled next to her, splendidly nude, his skin sliding against hers, she stroked the chiseled planes of his face. "If only . . ."

"What?"

"We hadn't met under the circumstances we did."

"Hey, I believe in happy endings." He took her hand and kissed each finger. "Ask Syd."

He nuzzled the length of her arm, her shoulder, the slope of her breast.

"Mmm. A romantic. I like that." She hesitated a moment, but had to ask, "Do you think *our* ending can be happy? I mean, with Nora gone and your father—"

"I don't have a father," he quickly interrupted, his lips stopping their seduction of her. "He's dead to me."

She covered his mouth with her fingers. "Shh, don't say that."

But he twisted his head away. "I can't condone what he did, and I can't forgive him."

"That's anger speaking, Dakota, not you, not your heart," Honor said, stroking him with a soothing rhythm. "Everyone is entitled to a mistake."

"Not one this big."

Her brow furrowed at this too-quick condemnation of a father she knew he loved. "Promise me you won't do or say anything rash you might regret later. That you'll give this some time before making any decisions."

Dakota made no verbal promises and stilled her demands with more kisses and a hand meant to distract by exploring her hip and thighs. But he couldn't stop her from thinking about everything that still could go wrong...for both of them.

Even as her body stirred to life in a hot, sweet rush, an incredible sadness welled in her heart.

She thought of what had brought them together. Her daughter's kidnapping. Her being forced to do something illegal. Dakota had referred to her "crime" earlier. The word stuck. He needed her now, but how would he feel about her later when he had time to think about what she had done?

When he had time to sit in judgment on her as he was so anxious to do with his father?

She had no regrets. She would do it all again for her daughter, Honor thought fiercely. She would lie, cheat, steal...whatever it took to save her child. She *would* see Nora safe, no matter the consequences to herself. It tore her apart to know that Dakota undoubtedly wouldn't understand that kind of blind love. He was a man who saw only the blacks and whites in a world filled with shades of gray.

He'd turned away from one woman who had disappointed him.

A little voice inside her whispered she would never be good enough for him, either.

For the moment, she ignored the warning, reveled in the feel of his naked body against hers. She needed him as she'd never needed another man. She was eager to be joined with him, and for those few moments of ecstasy, be the center of his universe as surely as he was the center of hers.

The water bed rocked gently as they explored each other with intimate kisses and even more intimate touches. Her fingers played across his ribs and dipped low until they met a ridge in his side made by some terrible scar.

"What in the world...?"

"I had an accident when I was a kid," he whispered against her hair. "Twenty-seven stitches."

She slid down so she could kiss the old hurt away, only wishing she could heal the new, deeper wounds caused by his father.

Dakota's attitude toward his parent was telling. This was a person he'd loved for thirty-some years and yet he was willing to put the older man aside. The knowledge made her ache even as she surrendered to physical pleasure.

Dakota might think he was in love with her, but Honor wasn't at all certain that would be enough. She did the only thing she could to assuage the hurt of future separation. She got closer while it was still possible. She made love to him, touching every inch of his beautiful muscular body, all the while fearing that, in the end, she would be found lacking, not good enough, unable to touch his soul.

FOG SWIRLED AROUND HER ankles, fingered its way up her calves as she anxiously tried to make the image she so wanted to see appear. Her heart pumped madly as did her legs while she ran the length of the deserted pier.

Alone, no Dakota at her side. He'd left her to her own devices.

"Nora!" she screamed, the fog effectively cutting the plea dead mere yards from where she stopped and listened.

No response.

Eerie. Everything. The night. The drizzle. The fog-shrouded setting. Her mind set. She shivered, huddled in the quilt that she'd wrapped around herself for warmth. Light rain made the smell of fish overwhelming in contrast to the muted lap of water against the pilings.

And then she heard it: a tiny cry piercing the thickness of the night.

"Mommy!"

"Nora! Honey, where are you?" Honor called, trying to keep the desperate edge from bleeding through her words.

She whipped around, searching, but the fog had risen, cloaking the area in its ghostly white shroud.

Running. Getting nowhere. Bare feet slapping against damp wood. Drizzle sliding down skin already slick with the sweat of fear.

"Mommy!"

Closer now.

Honor's breath came sharply, an edge of panic threatening to suck it away.

And then she saw her child.

Nora turned to face her, fear in the great green eyes that nearly swallowed her little face. Tufts of copper hair stood out around her head on one side, a messy copper braid hung from the other. The drizzle turned into a steady downpour, flattening the fine baby hair around chalk-white round cheeks and making those eyes blink rapidly. Short arms outstretched, Nora implored her mother for help.

Honor ran and ran, but no matter how much speed she sought, her daughter was pulled farther away even faster, as if by invisible hands, until Nora disappeared altogether into the fog.

The blast of a nearby ferry horn made her start.

"A-a-h-h!"

Honor sat up quickly and swayed sickeningly with the movement of the water bed as she tried to orient herself, quilt twisted around her naked body. She looked down at herself. How curious—her skin was dry, yet she still heard the rain.

And the blast of a nearby telephone.

Blinking, she took a good look at her surroundings. Driftwood and shells. A mural behind her. Dakota's bedroom. The rain sound clarified into the needlelik spray of a shower. She'd been asleep, having a nightmare.

But the telephone's ringing was real.

"Dakota?"

No doubt he couldn't hear her in the shower. She scrambled over the rocking bed to the nightstand where she picked up the receiver.

"Hello? This is Dakota Raferty's telephone."

"I know whose phone this is, Ms. Bright," came a familiar synthesized voice.

Her heart leaped to her throat. "My daughter! Where is she?"

"All in good time."

"You've had enough time. Now I want my child as promised!"

"When you give us what we want, Ms. Bright. Meanwhile, your daughter will be kept at a safe house."

"Don't make me do this," she pleaded. "I got what I could."

"Not enough. Your priorities are confused. Having close relations with Dakota Raferty doesn't say much for your loyalties. Of course, perhaps you mean to use him to your best advantage."

Honor's chest squeezed at that, for she knew what was coming. "What?" she whispered, already dreading the confirmation.

"You can seduce from your lover what you need to get your daughter back." The electronic chuckle was unnatural and unnerving, like a scraper against an icy windshield. "And this time, you'd better produce enough of what we need to break him."

Break the man she loved?

"I can't do that to him," she said, tears welling in her eyes because she knew it was a lie. To get Nora back, she could do anything. No choices here. She'd face the consequences and try to undo the damage later.

"Then your daughter will die!" the inhuman voice told her. "Your choice is simple—protect your lover and lose your child, or meet my demands. *Tonight*. You have only one more chance to get me what I want. I'll call you at your place in a couple of hours with delivery instructions."

"What if I can't get exactly what you want?"

"Good luck . . . for little Nora's sake."

The line went dead.

Tears rolled down Honor's cheeks as she sat there, receiver to her ear, staring. She wasn't sure how long she was paralyzed into inaction, but gradually, she realized she no longer heard the shower. Quickly replacing the phone and drying her cheeks and eyes, she ducked under the cover, and not a moment too soon.

The bathroom door opened. "Hey, sleepyhead," Dakota growled, briskly towel drying his hair, a matching deep green towel slung low on his hips. "I'm starving. How about you?"

"Mmm."

Honor averted her eyes from the bit of scar that showed above the towel. She could hardly avoid the magnificence of Dakota's naked chest as he sat on the water bed's frame, and yet she couldn't bear to look at him after what they'd shared . . . knowing what she had to do to him.

Think of Nora, she told herself.

She had to put the four-year-old child, who couldn' defend herself, first.

The thought strengthening her resolve, Honor met Dakota's gaze without blinking. "I could use some food, as long as I don't have to cook it."

"Well, then, I guess I'll have to do the cooking."

Quickly making her plan, Honor realized she would have to get Dakota out of the apartment so she could work on his safe. She'd seen him open it the day he'd put the files inside. Her eyesight was razor sharp. She'd seen and memorized the combination even while hoping she'd never have to use the knowledge.

She ran playful fingers up his damp arm. "Why cook when you can get carry-out and spend the extra time doing more fun things?"

He stared at the nails teasing his flesh. "Keep that up and I'll lose interest in food altogether."

She snapped her hand away. Confusion showed in his expression. To soothe any suspicions, she said, "I never try to keep a man from his food. That would be cruel. How about some more of those fried oysters?"

His eyebrows shot up. "They're only an aphrodisiac when they're raw."

"Then get some of those, too. By the time you get back, I'll be cleaned up and refreshed," she lied.

But how could she keep Dakota from following her home before she got the call to make the delivery? She worried about the logistics while he pulled on clean underwear, decidedly unconservative leopard-skin prints. She watched, fascinated, unabashed in her eagerness to store up memories that would have to last a lifetime.

Once Dakota learned what she would do to save her child, he would put her from him as he had Maureen and his father.

"Aren't you going to get in the shower?" he asked, pulling on a pair of old jeans, comfortably worn in the seat and ripped at the knees.

He looked so desirable, he made her heart ache.

"Can't I watch?" she asked, adding the right teasing note to her voice. "It'll take you a while to get down to the pier and back, right?"

She was wondering exactly how much time she had.

"Half an hour, maybe a little longer. I promise I'll hurry."

Tempted to tell him not to, Honor changed her mind lest he get suspicious. Instead, she pulled the quilt around her and awkwardly rolled from the water bed. Dakota laughed at her struggle. She'd lost the quilt in the process. He picked it up and sheltered her back, but pressed her naked front against him for a long, lingering kiss.

And returning the kiss, Honor felt like Judas must have, though her reward would be far more precious than a purse of silver.

Dakota pulled away, his expression a little puzzled. "Something wrong?"

Realizing her heart hadn't gone into the embrace, Honor covered, thanking her stars she was a terrific actress. She smiled coyly, took the quilt from him and wrapped it securely around her.

"I'm starving and don't want to distract you from your errand of mercy."

The puzzled expression softened a bit, but he didn't seem quite convinced. And yet he said, "I'll hurry back."

Honor blew him a kiss and watched him head for the stairs, pulling a long-sleeved black T-shirt over his head.

She remained frozen to the spot while he descended the stairs. When she heard the apartment door open then close behind him, she propelled herself into action. She dropped the quilt and scrambled around the floor for the clothes that had been so carelessly tossed aside as a prelude to their eager lovemaking.

She was dressed in less than two minutes, was running down the stairs in three and had removed the painting from the wall safe in four.

Now that she was faced with the ultimate betrayal, Honor hesitated. She trembled inside, not only for her soon-to-be-lost relationship, but for Dakota himself, and for the men she didn't know, whom she could be placing in mortal danger.

But she had to do it, she assured herself. She had no choice.

Once she had Nora safe, she would tell Dakota and he would warn the men who had dared testify against the companies guilty of illegal fishing activities. He and Reynard Stirling and the authorities would figure out what to do, how to cover those who needed protection.

Everything would turn out all right in the end. It had to. She couldn't be responsible for another's life.

Her hand shook as she approached the dial. She took a deep breath and held it. Twice past zero to the right, stopping on twenty-six. *Click*. Once past zero to the left, with a stop on fourteen. *Click*. Right to thirty-nine. *Click*. Air flowed from her lungs in a grateful rush.

Thinking of Nora, Honor grasped the handle and jerked.

The safe swung open.

Adrenaline rushed through her as she reached for the contents. She had the files in her hands, was thanking

God that she'd been able to pull it off, when she heard the sound behind her. Whirling around, she pressed the precious information to her breast, which ached with sudden fear. She was so close to having succeeded.

So close.

"Why?" Dakota asked, the softly issued word belying his menacing expression as he closed the gap between them.

Chapter Thirteen

"How the hell could you do this to me?" Dakota demanded.

He stopped inches from where Honor stood straight and tall—defiant—even—as if she were daring him to strike her. He balled his fists at his sides. As far as he was concerned, she should be slinking in some corner like the traitorous snake she'd proven herself to be. The only visible sign that she was affected by his walking in on her before she'd had time to complete the theft was her unnatural pallor.

"How did you know?" she asked.

"I didn't, though I should have been suspicious, considering the way you were acting." He couldn't keep the bitterness he was feeling from his voice. "But you distracted me before I left and I forgot my wallet. Otherwise, you would have gotten away with it."

"Dakota—"

"Don't!"

He couldn't believe he'd opened himself to this kind of hurt again. He'd thought Maureen had taught him a well-learned lesson, that she had been the ultimate user, but Honor had gone his ex-fiancée one better. He should have been smarter, but he'd fallen for the actress anyway. He felt utterly and completely destroyed by her treachery, as surely as if she'd taken a knife to his heart.

"I thought I'd seen some slick moves in my time," Dakota said, shaking his head, "but this one beats them all. You came here pretending to need me, and all the while, you were planning to betray me."

"It wasn't like that."

"What was it like, then? Are you telling me this idea just came to you after I left—ten minutes ago?"

"No, while you were in the shower—"

"Ah, the shower. So that's when you figured out how you were going to double-cross me. You decided to get me out of the way, thinking I was so besotted after having had you that I wouldn't suspect." Another thought revolted him. "Did you really feel you had to sleep with me to ensure your daughter's safety?".

"Stop it!" Honor cried, her staunch facade finally cracking. "Stop it, please. Dakota, believe me, I came to you in all honesty tonight. I never meant this to happen. I slept with you because I love you. I didn't have any hidden motives. But when you were in the shower..." She paused a second, then, eyes filling with unshed tears, she continued, "They called me here and demanded I get them what they needed to ruin you."

"The kidnappers called here?" Dakota's anger faded enough for him to realize the consequences. "There's no question that they know how..." About to say "involved" he changed it to, "How much I know, then." And he didn't think Crawley had had enough time to spread the word of his father's visit.

"They told me this was my last chance, Dakota. They said she would die if they didn't get what they wanted. I had to do it. You never would have agreed—"

"You didn't give me that opportunity!" he shouted. "What if I had and you said no?"

"You didn't trust me." Did she really believe he would have let those bastards kill her child? He felt as if the knife had been thrust in his heart yet again. "Admit it!"

"You wouldn't agree to let me turn over those files before," she said defensively.

"Because I didn't want anyone else hurt."

"And you think I do? You think I could sleep at night if someone did get hurt . . . or worse? I just wanted to save my child." Though her voice didn't break, tears rolled down her cheeks. "Her life was more important than some ideal. As for the witnesses . . . I would have called you as soon as they gave Nora back to me. I wouldn't have given them the files unless they traded Nora directly, and then you would have had plenty of time to warn those men."

Honor's eyes were red, her face flooded with tears— and yet she still held herself together, glaring at him defiantly. Dakota wavered, was tempted to take her in his arms, but in the end, he wouldn't allow himself to give in to her. She was an actress, after all, and could have him believing the moon was made of cheese if she so chose.

"Stop the act!" he demanded. "How can you expect me to believe anything you tell me?"

"Because I'm telling you the truth. I swear it on my child's life. Dakota, please, I have to give them what they want. Don't you understand? They'll kill her." A sob finally caught in her throat and she choked out, "They'll kill my baby. Don't you love anyone enough that you could put yourself in my place?"

He loved *her* enough, but Dakota thought Honor would never know that. She'd breached the trust between them, a wound that wouldn't easily heal.

"I understand, Honor. And if only you would have trusted me, I would have given you the damn papers. I'm not a monster. I don't want anything to happen to Nora."

Uncertainty crossed her features. "But the men..."

"A little late to be thinking about them now, isn't it? I'll take these." He pulled the files from her grasp and went to the telephone. "We're going to play this *my* way, starting by protecting the witnesses now, before it's too late."

"No police!"

"You have nothing to say about how this is going to be handled," he said coldly. "But I'm not calling the police."

He punched out Reynard Stirling's home number. Two rings and the man himself answered.

"Reynard, Dakota here. It's time I told you what you've gotten yourself involved in because of me."

He did so with economy, his eyes never leaving Honor, who stood watching him, her face passive once more. Whatever she was feeling, he didn't know. He told himself he didn't care. He knew he was lying.

Satisfied that Reynard would see to the safety of the men they were about to expose, Dakota hung up and turned to Honor. "Now what?"

"I'm supposed to go home and wait for delivery instructions."

"Then let's go."

She retrieved her white jacket from the couch and slipped into it even as she crossed the living room. Holding on to the ransom, he silently followed, knowing that after tonight, his life would never be the same.

DECIDING THEY WOULD HAVE to use her car to make the trade, lest the kidnappers get suspicious, Honor drove. Dakota sat next to her, silent and unmoving as a stone statue. Having to concentrate on the route kept her emotions somewhat in balance. She was thankful for the darkness, felt as if she could hide herself in the night.

She wanted to tell Dakota how sorry she was that she hadn't put her trust in him to do the right thing. She wanted to tell him how much she loved him. Fearing he would believe neither, she, too, kept her peace.

In case anyone was watching the front of her house, she parked the car in the garage and approached via the rear entrance, Dakota waiting in the shadows until she unlocked the kitchen door. They had no sooner entered than the telephone rang.

"That can't be them, yet," she said, even as her heart raced her to the wall phone in the kitchen. Dakota was right beside her when she lifted the receiver. "Hello." She sounded breathless from excitement rather than exertion.

"Did you get them?" the electronic voice asked without preliminaries.

Dakota was listening from the other side of the instrument, his head touching hers. Honor tried to ignore him, concentrate on what she had to do, only hoping that Dakota wouldn't be so startled as to give her away.

"I have everything," she said.

"Good—"

"But," she interrupted quickly, "before I give the files to you, I want my daughter."

"Not possible."

"Make it possible."

Honor didn't know where she found the strength, but she hardened her voice. She would play a part. A tough, no-nonsense woman who took what she wanted out of life. She would lose herself in the character.

"Now listen, Ms. Bright—"

"No, *you* listen. I exchange the information for my daughter." The hand holding the receiver was starting to sweat, but she ignored the discomfort that threatened to ruin her ploy. "I swear if I don't see Nora, I'll light a match to the papers. And I'll bring all hell down on you, starting with the police."

The electronic laugh grated on her nerves. "You don't even know who I am."

"Perhaps not, but I'm getting close. More to the point, King Crawley does know who you are—" she took a deep breath for this one "—and, believe me, he won't want the kind of trouble I'll cause for him and his family if one hair on Nora's head is harmed!"

Suddenly remembering the bright copper braid in her pocket, Honor faltered. Dakota's steadying hand on her arm encouraged her to go on with her act.

"It's a little late for that," she corrected, "but you get my drift."

"Tough talk for someone who was pleading with me not to make you go through with this a short while ago."

Honor actually thought she recognized a thread of respect in the electronic voice. Certain Dakota had heard every word, she wondered what he was thinking.

"Pleading didn't work, did it?" she said softly. "You made me betray someone I very much care about, and he'll never forgive me. I have nothing left to lose."

"Except your daughter."

"But you won't harm her because I'm going to give you what you want," she said firmly. "Besides which, I swear to you on Nora's life that if something does happen to her, you won't be safe." She slowed her words and enunciated carefully for full effect. "You won't be able to hide from me. I will find you and I will find a way to destroy you. Believe that." Honor's word carried far more conviction than she was feeling. Her heart rate had accelerated alarmingly. "Now, where do you want me to meet you?"

"Underground Seattle at midnight," came the synthesized voice. The kidnapper named one of several possible entrances, assured her the door would be unlocked and gave her directions to the location. "And Ms. Bright . . . come *alone*."

The line went dead and Honor's gaze met Dakota's as he pulled away. The tough character faded and she was hit with a bolt of tension that threatened to make her vomit. She was slicked with sweat, and her hand was shaking so hard she couldn't hang up.

Dakota took the receiver from her and slid it into place. "Don't get any ideas about making this drop without me," was the first thing out of his mouth.

Ire raised, Honor cried, "You heard what he said! If I don't come alone—"

"They won't know."

She looked at him stupidly, unable to make sense of his words. "What are you talking about?"

"The underground area is sometimes used for shelter by street people. I've seen where they get in," Dakota told her. "There's a little-known entrance just down the street from my building. I'll dress like one of them and find my way down there before you. That way, I can stay close to you without being recognized."

Honor almost believed he insisted because he cared, but she knew better. She'd killed all feeling in him when she'd opened his safe. He merely wanted to be there to catch the criminals in the act.

"Dakota, I understand why you want to learn who these people are, to see them punished for what they're trying to do to you, but think about Nora."

He gave her a peculiar grimace that he was quick to hide. "I *am* thinking about Nora . . . and about you."

A spark of hope kindled in her and as quickly died when he turned away.

"We have enough time to formulate a plan," he said. "Have you ever seen Underground Seattle?"

"Never. I know it's a tourist attraction in the Pioneer Square area."

"It's not like any other tourist attraction around After a fire destroyed much of early Seattle, streets near the waterfront area were rebuilt above the old, leaving blocks of subterranean stores and sidewalks. They were used that way for years, then, eventually were abandoned and even forgotten. It's a warren down there, not all prettied up. Tours go through a few blocks of the safe parts. My guess is that our friends know about the not-so-safe parts, as well."

In the end, Honor was glad she wouldn't be going after her child alone.

The weather reflected her anxiety, clouds covering the sky, drizzle making the cool night miserable. On the way to Pioneer Square, they drove past an outdoor soup kitchen where a group of homeless men still hung about though the volunteers had cleared out long before. Dakota paid one of the men for his torn, grayed jacket and a sweat-stained brimmed hat. From another, he purchased a lighter and an open bottle of whiskey in a paper sack.

Honor held her breath against the odor when he got back into the car and handed her what she needed to torch the papers, if necessary. Following his instructions, she dropped Dakota off half a block from the entrance he'd told her about.

"Take it nice and easy," he told her as he leaned in the still-open door. "We're going to pull this off."

She gave him a forced smile. When he started to pull back, she quickly said, "Dakota, be careful...and thanks."

He didn't say a word, merely walked off into the rising fog, the collar of the filthy jacket pulled up around his neck. Honor watched him jog down the stairs toward the entrance, then waited awhile longer until she was certain he was inside. She went on, circling the area for several minutes to give him time to make his way to the correct location. She only hoped he hadn't over-estimated his knowledge of the underground area and that the small flashlight he carried would be enough to guide him through the maze.

Parking near the designated entrance, she shut off the engine and waited for her vital signs to steady. Now that the time had come, she was more nervous than she'd thought possible. She couldn't screw this up. She had to pull this off for Nora's sake.

Grabbing the envelope filled with the files—and taking hold of her courage—Honor left the car.

Despite the pep talk she'd given herself, legs like rubber took her toward the entrance. Her breath came in short gasps as she grabbed hold of the rusting railing and looked down at the cement stairs that would take her below street level. Drizzle coated her, sent tiny rivulets sliding down her neck. A chill enveloped her when she realized what could be waiting down there for her and she pulled her white jacket closer around her chest.

The rubber soles of her shoes whispered along the staircase. Each took her one step farther from reality. She wished she had a weapon, but all she'd thought to bring besides the ransom was her mini mag light. At least she'd be able to see, she assured herself. That was something.

Puddles formed on the bottom landing. She squished through them, put a hand out to the metal door. Sucking in a long, deep breath, she opened the entrance to another world, one filled with unknown dangers.

The air was damp and suffocating as the door creaked closed behind her, cutting her off from the real world. A long way down the dark subterranean corridor, a single bulb glowed, but all around her, darkness reigned. Honor took a step forward, the uneven ground beneath her feet making her jerk to a stop. She flicked on the mini mag. Cobblestones. The original street.

She veered toward the distant bare bulb as she'd been instructed. Tension oozed through her with every careful step. Her own breath coming sharp and short was magnified to her ears, and she feared she would miss a child's small cry.

Nora. She would see her daughter within minutes. The thought gave her the strength to go on.

Flashing the mini mag in a sweeping arch, on the left, she illuminated what had once been a shop, the glassless window allowing her to see inside. Nothing but rubble, and toward the back, the remains of another room that presented an incongruous sight—a raised platform with a seatless, filthy white toilet bowl, a rotting wooden flush tank overhead. To the right, a building was boarded up, rotting crossed timbers preventing anyone from entering.

The sound of water made her look up. Overhead, a series of thick, pop-bottle-bottom pieces of glass formed an archaic type of skylight. One that leaked. Rain slid through several cracks, sending a shower to the underground street. Underfoot, the cobblestones became slippery. Dangerous.

Heart in her throat, Honor slowed down and stopped before she got to the small pool of light created by the bare bulb. She would use the dark to her own advantage. Hugging the envelope to her chest, she kept the mini mag in that hand and turned it off. With her free hand, she pulled the lighter from her jeans pocket."

"Are you there?" she called, listening intently.

Her voice echoed eerily along the cavernous underground. Her senses sharpened. The acrid smell of urine permeated the dank, humid air. Scrabbling and tiny squeaks told her she was definitely not alone. Rats! Shuddering, she tried not to think about the ugly rodents. Instead, she concentrated on Dakota, wondering where in this secret world he had hidden himself.

Footsteps came from beyond the light. At first, she thought it was Dakota. But, while dressed like an indigent, the man who stopped at the edge of the golden pool was the one who'd collected the documents at the soup-kitchen line. He was even wearing the same billed cap.

"Where's Nora?" she asked softly. She could hardly hear her own words for the rush in her head.

She could tell he was straining to see her, but he couldn't quite place her in the dark.

"Do you have the documents?" he asked.

"I have them."

"Let's see."

It took everything she had not to beg and plead. "Let me see my daughter first," she demanded firmly, once more wondering what had happened to Dakota.

The man signaled to someone behind him. A homeless woman stepped toward him. The one in the long winter coat! Honor tried to see beyond the stringy brown hair and glasses, but didn't recognize the woma who was carrying a sleeping child. Light touched bright red hair, baby fine, shorn of both braids.

"Nora!" Honor cried softly, her eyes and throat hurting with barely repressed emotion.

"Where are the papers?"

Honor snapped on the mini mag to show him the envelope . . . and the lighter.

"You bring her to me and I'll give you what you want."

"Sorry. It's our turn to make the demands," the man said. "Bring the documents to the middle of the lit area and set them on the street. I'll look them over and if they're what you promised, we'll let your daughter go."

"No!"

He signaled to the woman, who started to back away.

"Wait!" Honor cried, taking several steps forward.

What to do? She was so close . . . she could almost touch her child. Could she trust them if she did as he demanded? Or once again, would they renege on their end of the bargain? She could put the envelope down, and while the man collected it, the woman could very well disappear with Nora.

If only she were sure Dakota was there somewhere!

Not knowing what else to do, Honor said, "We all walk to the center together."

Even though the man and woman stepped forward when she did, Honor knew they had the edge. Two against one. She wasn't strong enough to fight them both for her child! Fright made her breath come so shallow that her chest began to hurt.

The man stopped a yard away and held out his hand. "The documents."

Already mentally tracing her way back to the street, Honor started to hold out the envelope...then tossed it to the ground several feet to the side. Glaring at her, the man stooped to pick it up. Honor waited until he was bent over before she grabbed for Nora, dropping both mini mag and lighter in the process.

"No you don't!" the other woman shrilled.

She pulled the small, warm body away even as Honor got both hands on her daughter. Not about to give up without a fight, she moved with the woman, anchoring her hands firmly around the child's waist. At the same time, she lashed out with her foot, catching the woman's leg.

"A-a-h! Vin-n-y!"

Realizing the voice sounded familiar, Honor experienced victory as Nora's back pressed against her chest. A short second later, she felt as if her scalp were on fire. The man had a handful of her hair and was twisting mercilessly. Still, she didn't let go. But, as the woman tightened her hold on Nora, the man jerked again, making Honor lose both her balance and her grip.

She screamed at them as she fell to the cobblestones. "Give me my child! You promised!"

"Bastard!"

This from Dakota, who rushed out of the dark, clipping the other man with his shoulder. They both went down, rolling over the wet subterranean street, throwing punches, many of which went wild.

"Mommy?" came a sleepy little voice over the grunts and groans of the two men.

Honor whipped her head around, but Nora and the woman had disappeared into the darkness. She was o her feet in a second, picking up the miniature flashlight that kept flickering. Obviously, it had been damaged in the fall. After glancing back at Dakota, who seemed to be holding his own, she flew after Nora.

Her feet slapped against the cobblestones as she ran, half blind. The small light flashed on and off with every other jolting step. But no matter how fast she ran, she couldn't catch up to them. Nora was crying now, and Honor thought she would go out of her mind with the sound.

"Nora, honey, I'm here!" she yelled.

"Mommy! Wanna go home!"

The sound came from a cross street she almost missed because the light had gone out. Following Nora's sobs, Honor veered right, but not sharp enough to miss a support beam holding up that section of the street above. Slamming into it at full steam, she bounced to the side, lost her footing and fell heavily against a nearby wall. Bright lights ricocheted inside her head and angry little screeches magnified around her as rats scurried over her body!

And in the distance, Nora's wail was cut off by the slam of a door. Knowing she had blown it, fearing she'd never catch up to them now, Honor whacked a rat off her shoulder, pushed herself to her feet and went after them in the dark. Her light flashed on in time for her to find the exit door.

She jerked the handle.

Locked! Dear God, and she had been so close!

"Nora!" she cried frantically, slapping the fist holding the mini mag against the metal. The light went dead, but she continued hitting the door over and over again as if by the little strength she had left, she could force it open. "Nora!"

Hands went around her shoulders, making her jump and cry out.

"It's me."

Dakota's voice. She turned and slumped into the shelter of his hands, fearful of getting any closer because she couldn't stand the rejection that was sure to follow.

"Thank God you're all right," he said, his own flashlight revealing the concern twisting his features. And then, seeming suddenly awkward, he let go. "I'm sorry about Nora. I should have acted sooner, but I was afraid the woman might disappear with her."

"As she did. What about the man?"

Dakota seemed embarrassed. "He got away. I almost had him, but those cobblestones can be slippery."

"The rain," she said woodenly, her universe just having crashed around her.

"I fell and he got away... *with* the documents."

"I made such a mess of things," she muttered miserably. "I was just trying to save my daughter. I failed her. I failed the men whose names are on those affidavits. I failed you." A deep shudder wracked her body. "My God, what are we going to do?"

"Get out of here, for starters."

He placed a passive hand on her arm and used his flashlight to guide them back the way they came. Her mini mag was now useless, so she jammed it into a jacket pocket. The responding crinkle puzzled her.

She pulled out the rumpled paper from her pocket. About to toss it away, she glanced at the printed side, which she could just make out by the glow of Dakota's light. Her eyes widened and she stopped dead in her tracks. Her heart was beating so wildly, she thought it would burst.

"What?" he asked.

She held out the flyer. "I forgot all about this. It makes sense," she said. "All of it. Come on!"

With that, she grabbed his arm and set off at a jog, only hoping to God that she was right about where they'd been holding her daughter!

Chapter Fourteen

"Are you going to explain this?" Dakota asked, waving the flyer as they sped through the night. "Or are you going to make me play twenty questions?"

"The flyer put everything I've learned into perspective," Honor said, her attention split between driving and explaining. "I guess I've been hanging on to tidbits of information subconsciously."

"Like what?" Dakota asked, sounding impatient.

"Like last time I talked to Nora, she said something about the other kids being okay, but she wanted to be with me. I assumed this Mrs. Murphy had children of her own. And then the kidnapper said my daughter was in a safe house. That was at your place earlier, when I got the last call. Maybe the kidnapper was trying to be funny—maybe the information just slipped out—but I guess it stuck in the back of my mind."

"Safehouse," Dakota said, making it one word. He was looking at the flyer listing the newest location.

"Right. Safehouse as in a shelter for homeless women and children. Where better to hide a child than with others?" Honor asked, irony in her tone. "I took that flyer from a volunteer at the outdoor soup kitchen, but

I never looked at it until I found it in my pocket a while ago. Thank God I did. It clarified things for me."

More things than she was willing to discuss at the moment. She had her suspicions about the identity of the outsider who was running this operation for Crawley. The things she'd learned were falling into place like the pieces of an intricate puzzle—but the picture was still a bit fuzzy.

"You must be right about the Safehouse," Dakota said. "Fast thinking. Now, if only they're confident enough to think we haven't figured it out and return there with Nora."

Honor couldn't get over how normal he sounded, as if he hadn't caught her at the safe. And in the underground, she'd imagined he'd wanted to wipe away the memory but couldn't. Dakota had set some lofty standards for himself, and she appreciated that. If only he weren't so rigid, so unforgiving. Honest with herself, Honor knew that to believe otherwise was wishful thinking.

"I'm sorry you were involved in this plot," Dakota said, his words heavy with regret. "I feel as if it were my fault somehow."

Honor took a deep breath. "For what it's worth, I'm sorry I didn't trust you earlier tonight. You're the only man I've ever been able to depend on. I should have known better than to think you would let me down."

Dakota didn't respond to that, fueling Honor's disappointment. Though she knew she had ruined what might have been a future together, she had hoped they could at least be on friendly terms when this nightmare was over.

Then, again, as they approached the address of the new Safehouse listed on the flyer, she had other things on her mind—like whether or not she was taking them on a wild-goose chase.

"We're here," she said, pulling over to the curb on the other side of the street and shutting off lights and engine.

In a part of town that was far from opulent, the building looked as if it had been some kind of government-funded recreation hall in the past. Most of the windows were dark, as well they should be, considering the hour.

"You really think we're going to be able to walk in there and find Nora?" Dakota asked.

"I thought we could pretend we're looking for shelter for the night."

"I'm dressed for the part," he said, "but who would believe you were homeless?"

Honor looked down at the once white pants and jacket, which were now various shades of gray and black from her falls in the underground.

"I don't think I'll have a problem convincing whoever answers the door that I'm a woman in trouble."

"If no one recognizes you." Dakota removed the hat with the sweat-stained brim he'd bought earlier. "Here, let's hide that telltale hair under this."

Expecting him to hand over the hat, Honor was startled when he reached for her. His fingers slid under the heavy hair on her neck, leaving a trail of gooseflesh in their wake. His touch brought back memories that would last her a lifetime. As if he, too, felt the intimate connection, he quickly grabbed the thick tresses and wound them around his hand, then held the twisted mass against her scalp while positioning the hat.

"Your face is too clean," he said softly, rubbing his blackened fingers over one cheek and along the opposite jaw. He studied the effect. "That's better."

Honor stared in amazement, certain Dakota was about to say more. She tried to read his expression, but that was impossible in the dim light.

And then he pulled away. "Let's go."

They crossed the street to the shelter together, Dakota giving her an encouraging squeeze before they reached the entrance. A mass of confused emotions threatened to paralyze her; Honor was hard-pressed to pull herself together. Only the thought of her daughter crying out to her in the subterranean city gave her the necessary strength to proceed with a manufactured confidence.

Still, it was Dakota who rang the bell, for the windowed front door was locked. A moment later, a middle-aged woman with her salt-and-pepper hair clipped back from her moon face came to the entrance and stared out at them from the other side of the glass.

"Open the door, please!" Honor begged, grateful for Dakota's silent support.

His hand was square in the middle of her back, giving her strength. She was sure he could feel the rapid beat of her heart.

Cautiously, the woman opened the door a bit, planting herself firmly in the open space. "Can't put you folks up for the night. We don't allow men, anyhow. Only women and kids. But we're full up. Besides, it's past curfew." She shook her head at Honor. "You would of had to show by ten, honey."

"I'm not looking for a bed," Honor said, anxiety practically pouring out of her now that she was so close. "I'm looking for my daughter. She was ki—"

"Wandered away," Dakota quickly interrupted, sliding his hand around Honor's waist and giving her a warning squeeze. "She was playing with some other homeless children."

"Right," Honor croaked, realizing she'd almost said *kidnapped*. She gave Dakota a grateful look before coming back to the woman. "I turned around and she was gone. You know how fast kids can be. I figured maybe one of the other homeless women took her out of kindness."

The woman opened the door more fully, but all Honor could see beyond her was a hallway and a half dozen doors, only one of which was open—the small office the woman had been using.

"I'm sorry about your little girl, but I can't say as she's here. No one reported a lost child."

"Maybe they wouldn't. Couldn't I come in and look?"

"And disturb everybody? I should say not," the shelter worker said firmly. "These women have a difficult time putting their kids down for the night."

Just then, one of the other doors opened—a toilet—and a blonde carrying a flaxen-haired little girl crossed the hallway. She glanced toward the entrance and stopped in surprise. Honor recognized Andrea, the young woman she had befriended at the soup-kitchen line. But now she looked clean and free of some of the anxiety that had been wearing on her when they'd talked.

"Honor," Andrea said, coming closer. Her pretty face lit up. "Are you here for the night?"

Realizing Dakota had started in surprise at the use of her name, Honor sneaked a hand back and pressed it to his so he wouldn't say anything.

"I was just trying to find my little girl. She wandered off earlier and I was hoping she might be here."

"You're going to let her look, aren't you, Mrs. Murphy?" Andrea asked.

Triumph shot through Honor and she had difficulty not whooping with joy. Mrs. Murphy *had* to be the woman Nora had mentioned. This was the place!

If only Nora were here now.

If only Honor could get in to find out.

If only she could make everything right for herself and Dakota.

"Please," she begged, not having to use her acting skills this time. "Can't I just take a look? I promise I'll do my best not to disturb anyone."

"I can vouch for her," Andrea said. "She's okay. She helped me out the other night and I owe her."

The seemingly implacable Mrs. Murphy finally gave way. "All right. But only you." She frowned at Dakota and reiterated, "No men."

"I'll wait out here," Dakota promised. Then, to Honor, he whispered, "If you need any help, all you have to do is yell."

Honor gave him a nervous smile before entering the shelter.

"I don't have time to go on some wild-goose chase," Mrs. Murphy said as she closed and locked the front door. "I've got paperwork to finish. You can look, but quietly, and don't flick on any ceiling lights. There's dim emergency lights in every room so the children won't be afraid. It'll have to do."

"I'm sure it'll be enough."

"I'll help you," Andrea insisted, shifting Kathy to her other hip. The little blonde didn't waken, merely hugged her mother tighter. "What does your daughter look like?"

"She has bright copper..." About to say *braids,* Honor caught herself. "Hair. Kind of short and wispy. She's four. Her name is Nora."

"There are three rooms filled with cots. Let's try this one first," Andrea said, moving to the closest. "You go down the aisle to the right, I'll take the left."

Honor nodded and with a lump in her throat and an ache in her chest, entered. Quietly, she passed among the cots, taking her time to check every small form carefully. One mother who was still awake, drew her little boy to her possessively. Honor tried to smile, but she couldn't.

She wanted to cry, not for herself, but for them.

Seeing so many helpless children without homes broke her heart. Some women, like Andrea, had only one. Others, more burdened, had as many as five.

At the end of the line, Honor stopped and looked around in disappointment. The blonde shook her head. The two women headed back for the door more quickly this time.

They repeated the process with the second room, then the third. But Nora wasn't among the other children.

So they'd brought her elsewhere, Honor thought dispiritedly. Where? And how in the world was she going to find her?

Back in the hall, Honor gave Andrea a grateful smile, even though her heart was breaking. "Thanks."

"I'm sorry we didn't find her. I'll keep my eyes open for her tomorrow, though," Andrea promised. "Is there somewhere I can reach you?"

About to give the young woman her home number—what could it hurt?—Honor practically stopped breathing when she heard a sound from behind one of the doors they hadn't opened.

A child was sniffling as if she'd been crying.

And a thrill shot through Honor. "Listen."

Before she could move to check out the room, Mrs. Murphy left her office and wedged herself between Honor and the door. "I think it's time you left," she said firmly.

NOT CONTENT TO REMAIN waiting outside the front door with his hands tied while Honor was able to take action, Dakota purposefully circled the old building to check things out, not even knowing what he was looking for.

A way to assuage his guilt for saying the things he had to Honor, perhaps?

Because he loved her so, he'd had every right to be angry and disillusioned when he'd caught her at the safe, but he never should have accused her of sleeping with him for her daughter's sake. That had been a low blow. And he'd dug himself in deeper when he hadn't been able to accept her at her word. Why hadn't her denial been good enough for him?

Had Maureen soured him to all women, made him forever suspicious and unforgiving?

Or was his own nature at fault?

He remembered Honor asking him to think carefully before cutting his father out of his life. He hadn't promised he would. And she knew all about his break-up with Maureen. Dakota knew she felt the same as his ex-fiancée about his delineation between right and wrong with no in-betweens.

No wonder she had doubted him long enough to steal the files. She'd had a preconceived notion of how he would respond because he'd given her just cause more than once.

And she hadn't chosen to commit an act that was unethical, if not downright criminal, for her own gain, Dakota reminded himself. She would do anything to protect her child. He wondered if Honor had even a fraction of that special feeling for him. Catching her in the act had been painful, but not painful enough to make him stop loving her.

So the question was, what was he going to do now?

About to round the rear of the building, Dakota stopped short and melted into the shadows. Several cars were parked in back, including a Plymouth whose license plate read HOTSHOT. So the kidnappers were here! Not just Nora, but the criminals, as well.

That meant Honor and Nora were in danger!

When he peered around the corner of the building once more, Dakota caught sight of movement between the vehicles. Looking around furtively was a woman Dakota knew only too well.

Karen Lopinski!

An odd kind of triumph threaded through him at the knowledge. He'd suspected the reporter from the first, when she'd so conveniently run into him and Honor. That he'd begun to think otherwise was understandable, considering the stress of the last several days.

He watched as Lopinski dashed from sight, then he listened intently to make sure she wasn't coming his way. After making certain no guard patrolled the area, he slipped around back and, finding the window the reporter had used to get into the building—she used a discarded milk crate to reach the sill—he picked another so he wouldn't run into her until he was ready. Realizing Honor might not be so lucky, he climbed inside the near-dark room.

His feet hit the floor of a dormitory where children and their mothers were sleeping—all except for one woman, who sat bolt upright at his entrance, sheet pressed to her chest. She looked as if she were ready to scream.

"Please, don't," Dakota pleaded in a whisper as he passed her. "A child's life depends on it."

The too-thin woman watched him, wide-eyed and openmouthed, but set off no alarm. Dakota moved to the door and was about to open it when he heard raised voices on the other side, Karen Lopinski's not among them. Wondering what on earth was going on now, he chose to stay right where he was until he was certain he could help rather than do some irreparable damage.

"I AM NOT LEAVING WITHOUT seeing the child in that room!" Honor stated, certain the child was Nora and that she wasn't alone. Honor feared her daughter would be spirited off if she didn't get in there fast.

"That's a very disturbed little girl," Mrs. Murphy said. "She has delusions. She was so bad today we had to separate her from the others, put her in an office. You'd just upset her further."

"Not as upset as I'll be if I don't see her," Honor said, trying to stay in control.

"I've been patient, but enough is enough. You get out now or I'll call the police!"

"That's an excellent idea!"

"Mrs. Murphy, please," Andrea interceded.

The blonde had the shelter worker's attention. Honor used the fact to her advantage and shoved by the older woman.

"That's it! I'm calling the police now!" Mrs. Murphy cried as Honor burst through the door and stopped short at the sight before her.

"Mrs. Murphy..." Andrea's voice faded as she followed the other woman to her office.

"Nora," Honor whispered, hardly able to believe her eyes.

Sitting on a cot shoved in front of a desk, her tears being wiped away by Karen Lopinski, Nora turned at the sound of her mother's voice.

"Mommy! You came! You came!"

Nora pushed away from the reporter and lunged for her mother. Stooping, Honor caught the little girl and hugged her and covered her freckled face with kisses.

"Oh, peaches, I thank God you're all right."

And that she'd been right about where to find her child, even if she'd been wrong about the person holding her captive. Then she stood and faced Lopinski, who had risen from the cot and was staring at them both in amazement.

"You," Honor whispered as she rose, automatically stroking what was left of Nora's hair. "I don't believe it. I would have sworn..."

"What?" When Honor didn't answer, the reporter asked, "She really *is* your daughter, then?"

"Mommy—"

"Shh, honey. We'll talk in a minute." She hugged Nora to her side and gave the reporter a disbelieving look. "Don't try to play innocent here. It's too late for that."

Lopinski's eyes grew round. "I don't know what you're accusing me of. I've been working on a series about the homeless and I heard about this little girl who's been telling the other kids her mother is the famous movie star, Honor Bright. No one working here would let me see her. What's going on, Ms. Bright? How did your daughter end up in a shelter for the homeless?"

Honor frowned. Was Lopinski serious? Or was this a ploy to take her off her guard. With Nora hanging on to her hip, she started to back away. "I'll let the police fill you in."

"If the police knew what was going on," came a voice from behind her—the same familiar voice she'd heard in the underground.

Whipping around, Honor faced the woman she had been convinced was guilty until she'd seen Lopinski.

Wearing a long winter coat, a stringy-haired brown wig half stuffed into one of the pockets, Janet Ingel stepped through the doorway, a male companion in a billed cap directly behind her. He entered the room with palpable menace.

"Janet?" Lopinski said, sounding surprised. "What are you doing here at this time of night . . . and dressed like that?"

The truth finally hit Honor. "You two weren't working together?"

"Only on the stories I'm writing about the homeless."

"She asked me lotsa questions 'bout you and how come I was here, Mommy," Nora said, confirming Lopinski's allegation.

Janet gave the man she'd called Vinny a quick look, as if to ask, what now?

Honor tightened her grip on Nora, who hung on with one hand and stuck the thumb of the other into her mouth.

"If you hadn't been so stupid," said Janet, "Nora would have been home in the morning. Now I have to figure out what to do with all of you."

"That's easy." Vinny pulled out a gun.

Honor instinctively turned Nora's face away from the sight. "I knew you were ambitious and ruthless, Janet, but you can't really mean to murder all three of us."

"Murder?" Lopinski echoed from the other side of the cot. "If I'm going to die, the least you could do is tell me why. What's going on here?"

"You've just stumbled onto the story of a lifetime," Honor told her far more calmly than she was feeling.

She had to figure out how she was going to get them out of this situation! "This could make your career."

"If she lives long enough to write about it," Vinny said with a laugh that rose the hair along Honor's arms.

She stared at Janet, who shifted perceptibly. "You won't get away with this. If I could guess who was behind this plot, others will."

"You didn't know anything. You thought Lopinski was responsible."

From the corner of her eye, Honor saw movement— a door across the hall opening. She didn't dare glance that way. Perhaps whoever was there would realize they were being held at gunpoint and get help.

"Seeing her with my daughter threw me off for a moment. But I knew, Janet," Honor insisted, her pulse speeding when she realized Dakota had just slipped through the door. "I just didn't put it all together until tonight. Everything fits neatly, like a complex jigsaw puzzle."

As Dakota tiptoed across the hall, Honor kept her gaze glued on Janet for everything she was worth and prayed no one else would see him, not even Mrs. Murphy. Her grip tightened on Nora so that her daughter squealed. The sweat of fear rolled down her back and made her palms moist.

"If you know so much, tell me about it," Janet said, tight-lipped.

"You resented Dakota because of his background." He was getting closer, and she began to talk faster, couldn't help herself. "He had money and connections while you had to fight your way up. When did you get tired of fighting, Janet? When did you sell out to

Crawley so he would use his influence with NCSC to get you Andrew Vaughn's job?''

"Holy—"

The reporter's exclamation was cut off when Dakota burst through the door, knocking into Vinny's back. The gun went flying as the two men fell forward. Hanging on to Nora, Honor jumped to one side as the men crashed into the cot, knocking Lopinski over. Her head contacted the edge of the desk with a loud crack. She sank to the floor, looking dazed.

For Honor, the escape route was clear—finally, she could get Nora safely out of danger!

But as she moved to the door, as if watching in slow motion, she saw Janet dive for the fallen gun. Her heart thundered when the other woman grasped the large revolver in both hands and raised it toward Dakota as he rolled on top of Vinny. His back was exposed, a perfect target. Janet was getting up from the floor... hefting the gun into position... taking aim.

Honor shoved Nora out of the room. "Run, baby!" she cried. Then, "Janet!"

The other woman's concentration was broken for a second, long enough for Honor to intervene. Moving faster than she'd known she could, she rushed the other woman, who was still slightly bent over, and gave her a high kick that caught her in the rib cage. Though Janet lost her balance and started coughing, she held on to the damn gun!

Out in the hall, Nora was screaming bloody murder.

Focusing on Janet, Honor grabbed her arm and shoved it toward the wall just as the gun fired in a deafening explosion.

Simultaneously, in a silent explosion, she saw Vinny throw Dakota off him and go for his throat.

With a cry of frustration, Janet tried to rip her arm free, but Honor wouldn't let go. Taller and in better condition due to years of aerobics and dance training, she shoved the other woman to the floor and came down on top of her, knees first. Janet's grip went slack and Honor forced the weapon from her hand.

Out in the hall, Nora was still screaming, doors were opening, and women were talking excitedly.

Breathing heavily, Honor whipped around in time to see Dakota break Vinny's hold on his neck. He delivered a swift set of punches that made the man stagger and double over.

The room was filling with angry women, led by Mrs. Murphy. "What's going on here?" she demanded as the homeless women bravely got between the opponents. "The police are on their way!"

"No men allowed!" another woman cried. "No guns!"

"We have children here!"

Confusion reigned for a moment, and Janet scrambled to her feet, looking as if she might try to escape.

"I wouldn't if I were you," Honor said calmly, pointing the heavy weapon at the woman who'd kidnapped her child.

"You wouldn't use that."

No, she probably wouldn't . . . unless it was to save a life. But she was a great actress. "Only one way you're going to find out."

Janet swallowed hard and the energy visibly drained from her as she slumped against the wall.

"Honor, are you all right?" Dakota asked from across the room.

"Yes, now that Nora is safe from this witch. You'd better get her cohort over here so we can watch them both until the police arrive."

"Damn!"

Honor turned away from Janet to see Vinny ducking out of the open window. Dakota pushed through the crowd of angry women, but by the time he got to the window, an engine started, followed by a squeal of tires. Dakota looked as if he were planning to go after the man anyway.

"Dakota," Honor called. "Let him go. The police can take care of him." When he moved toward her, she handed him the gun. "I'm going to find my daughter."

"She's right here," Andrea piped up, her own daughter, Kathy, hanging on to one hand, Nora the other.

Honor sank to her knees and held out her arms. Nora flew into the embrace, wrapping small arms around her mother's neck as if she didn't intend to let go. Ever. Tears slipped down Honor's cheeks as she realized it was over. Her child—the most important person in her life—was safe.

If only she hadn't had to lose the man she loved and the only man she'd ever been able to count on to accomplish this miracle.

"Mommy, how come you're crying?" Nora asked.

"Because I'm happy to see you, peaches."

"Me, too! Can we go home now?"

"In a little while."

Honor realized everyone was staring at her—the women, Dakota and even Lopinski, who'd finally pulled herself together.

"I want the whole, unadulterated story," the reporter said.

"So do I," stated Mrs. Murphy. As she spoke, she turned to Dakota. "What's going on, and why do you have that gun pointed at Miss Ingel?"

Honor realized the two women knew each other, obviously through Janet's lobbying efforts for Safehouses. No doubt that's how she'd gotten Nora into this one.

"It's all right," a pale Janet said. "He has good reason."

Then the police arrived and cleared the nightgowned women out of the room. Andrea volunteered to watch Nora until Honor was ready to go.

Lopinski took avid notes while Dakota and Honor told their story. Honor was amazed and grateful when he avoided talking about some of the gray areas that might get her or his father into trouble.

The woman responsible for the kidnapping was silent throughout, claiming she wanted to see her lawyer before making her statement. The police searched her car, however, and found the salmon-fishing files, which they kept as evidence. After putting out an A.P.B. on Vinny, the police took Janet Ingel away.

"Thank God those files didn't get into the wrong hands," Honor said.

"Hey, how about giving me the rest of the story," Lopinski demanded. "The facts you left out in your statements. You owe me that much after almost getting me killed.''

"Like what?'' Honor asked, astonished anew at the woman's brass. She'd almost gotten *herself* killed by sneaking into the shelter.

"Like your relationship.'' The reporter was back in her bulldog mode. "You're still not going to deny you two have something going.''

To Honor's further amazement, Dakota said, "No, we're not, but that's all we're going to say.''

"Raferty, if you're planning to run for the U.S. Senate—''

"How did you know about that?''

Ignoring the question, she finished, "You should learn to work with the press.''

"Good night, Lopinski,'' Dakota growled.

"All right. I'm going.''

Before leaving them alone, she gave them a look that said she wasn't done with them.

Honor felt awkward as she watched Dakota pace the room. She wanted to know why he hadn't denied a relationship with her, but she couldn't get the words out.

Instead, she asked, "Did you have any idea it was Janet?''

He nodded. "Shocked the hell out of me when I saw Lopinski sneak around the back of the building. Wha about you?''

"Same here. I thought I had it solved and the thought I was goofy when I found Lopinski with Nora I had figured Kingfish Entitlements paid off NCSC s Zahniser would hire Janet. Remember that memo found? He mentioned a replacement already hired.''

Dakota looked in every direction but hers. "I wonder how deeply Zahniser is involved. I guess we'll know when Janet talks. I'm sure she'll trade whatever information she can to help herself."

Wishing he'd turn the conversation to one more personal, Honor nodded and followed his lead. "Remember when you figured our Freidman was contacting someone in the NCSC Building? You mentioned Zahniser, Vaughn and our friendly reporter. You didn't think about Janet because you brought her. I was kind of amazed, actually, to see her with you after that scene in your office."

"She volunteered to help me with my overload...knowing full well the salmon-fishing-industry project was what I was concentrating on." Dakota was silent a minute. "Vaughn knew she was going to be his replacement. That's what they were arguing about!"

"Everything fits perfectly, doesn't it?"

"Except one." He stopped pacing and finally met her gaze. "Janet was so close to me, she could have gotten those files herself. She didn't have to involve an innocent party."

Realizing he meant *her,* Honor was thoughtful. She had started out innocent, perhaps, but no more. And she couldn't believe Dakota referred to her in that way after what had gone on between them earlier.

"No doubt Janet didn't want to take the chance of being caught herself," she said. "Crawley taught her well. Maybe I was Zahniser's suggestion."

"We'll get at the truth if it's the last thing we ever do."

"We...?" she asked softly.

Dakota reached down and pulled Honor to her feet. "If you really love me, that is."

Her heart beat strongly for the umpteenth time that night. Instead of answering directly, she turned the focus back onto him. "I thought I killed any feelings you had for me."

He shook his head. "For a little while, I wished that were so. But I realized I needed to do some rethinking on how quickly I judge people. You made me face that fault in myself. No one is perfect, not even me. I was trying to figure out how to tell you that when all hell broke loose here. And then you had the opportunity to get Nora out of the shelter safely, but you put yourself in jeopardy to save me. I figured you must love me even if I acted like a jackass earlier."

She chose not to argue with him about the last. However, she did admit, "I do love you."

That's all Dakota needed to hear. He crushed her to him in an embrace that took her breath away. A kiss had never tasted so sweet . . . or held so much promise.

When he released her mouth, he suggested, "Let's pretend none of this ever happened. That neither of us made the mistakes we did. That we're two people meeting for the first time."

Pushing at his chest, she teased him. "Hey, stranger you'd better get your hands off me or I'll call a cop."

He didn't budge. "Well, maybe not for the first time. But what do you say? Can we start over?"

"Kiss me and you've got yourself a deal."

Epilogue

They started over the very next day when they took Nora for a picnic in Volunteer Park. They ate and talked and laughed together, and Honor was pleased when Nora seemed to like him immediately. He was thankful the little redhead was too young to realize the enormity of what had happened to her.

Someday, Honor would explain it all, he was sure, but for now, she was letting her daughter be a kid.

A really great kid.

If only their troubles were over....

"I see Joey," Nora said, pointing to one of her friends who was with some other children a short distance away. "Can I go say hi?"

Sure Honor was about to say no, Dakota prompted, "That would be okay, right, Mom?"

"All right. But just for a minute." Honor didn't take her eyes off Nora as she joined her friend, not even when Dakota wrapped an arm around Honor's waist and kissed her neck. She leaned in to him. "I know I can't be with her every moment for the rest of her life, but I can't help worrying."

"I've been worrying, too."

"About Nora?"

"About Sydney," he said. "She was gaslighted and almost killed. A little too much of a coincidence that something bizarre should happen to each of us in so short a time, don't you think?"

Honor glanced at him, but brought her attention back to her daughter as she shifted uneasily. "You're right."

"Crawley told Father his whole family was destroyed. His wife driven to try to commit suicide, his son professionally ruined, his daughter raped and now vanished. Sydney was almost driven to suicide."

"My God, that means—"

"She was a victim of Crawley's sick plot for revenge."

"Where will the man stop?" Honor asked, giving him a stricken look.

"I'm afraid he won't stop until he tries to destroy Asia," Dakota said, fear for his kid sister enveloping his heart.

"Then we have to warn her."

"Just what I was thinking."

Nora ran back to them as they packed up the picnic basket and headed for home, all holding hands, Nora in the middle, giggling. It wasn't too late for them, Dakota thought, but his fears weren't assuaged.

When and how was Crawley planning to strike out against Asia?

Harlequin Intrigue®

QUID PRO QUO

King Crawley, a man put behind bars for his sins against humanity, wants only one thing in life before he dies: revenge.

Driven by an insatiable need to destroy the Raferty family, he lashed out against Dakota Raferty in #163 SQUARING ACCOUNTS. A man whose honest nature fell prey to Crawley's madness, Dakota became an unsuspecting pawn in the game of deadly revenge.

Sydney Raferty was the first victim of Crawley's wrath. In #161 PUSHED TO THE LIMIT (May 1991), the first book in the QUID PRO QUO series, Sydney was driven to the brink of insanity . . . and fought her way back to reality with the love of Benno DeMartino.

Next month, don't miss the exciting conclusion of QUID PRO QUO, when Asia, the youngest of the Raferty siblings, is stalked by King Crawley. Asia must find a way to end the vendetta, and only one man can help—Dominic Crawley. But will the racketeer's son join forces with her to end his father's quest for vengeance? Don't miss #165 NO HOLDS BARRED (July 1991).

Coming soon
to an easy chair near you.

FIRST CLASS is Harlequin's armchair travel plan for the incurably romantic. You'll visit a different dreamy destination every month from January through December without ever packing a bag. No jet lag, no expensive air fares and *no* lost luggage. Just First Class Harlequin Romance reading, featuring exotic settings from Tasmania to Thailand, from Egypt to Australia, and more.

FIRST CLASS romantic excursions guaranteed! Start your world tour in January. Look for the special **FIRST CLASS** destination on selected Harlequin Romance titles—there's a new one every month.

NEXT DESTINATION:
FLORENCE, ITALY

 Harlequin Books

JTR7

This August, don't miss an exclusive
two-in-one collection of earlier love stories

MAN
WITH A PAST

TRUE COLORS

by one of today's hottest
romance authors,

Jayne Ann Krentz

Now, two of Jayne Ann Krentz's most loved books are available together in this special edition that new and longtime fans will want to add to their bookshelves.

Let Jayne Ann Krentz capture your hearts with the love stories, MAN WITH A PAST and TRUE COLORS.

And in October, watch for the second two-in-one collection by Barbara Delinsky!

Available wherever Harlequin books are sold.

Take 4 bestselling love stories FREE

Plus get a FREE surprise gift!

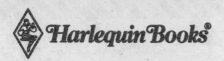 **Harlequin Books®**

GREAT NEWS...

HARLEQUIN UNVEILS NEW SHIPPING PLANS

For the convenience of customers, Harlequin has announced that Harlequin romances will now be available in stores at these convenient times each month*:

Harlequin Presents, American Romance, Historical, Intrigue:

>   May titles: April 10
>   June titles: May 8
>   July titles: June 5
>   August titles: July 10

Harlequin Romance, Superromance, Temptation, Regency Romance:

>   May titles: April 24
>   June titles: May 22
>   July titles: June 19
>   August titles: July 24

We hope this new schedule is convenient for you.

With only two trips each month to your local bookseller, you'll never miss any of your favorite authors!

*Please note: There may be slight variations in on-sale dates in your area due to differences in shipping and handling.

*Applicable to U.S. only.